# Death in a Pheasa[...]

The watchers moved slowly as cattle, and the ambulance men came through the crowd and slid the
stretcher into the back of the vehicle.

Aveyard was walking up the path and had
nearly reached the door when it opened. Dr. Samson stood talking to a man old enough to be the
father of the woman who'd been carried out.

"You got here quickly," the Doctor said, "I
only telephoned a couple of minutes ago and they
said you were out of radio contact . . ."

"My radio's on the blink. They're fixing it this
morning. I saw the ambulance. What is it . . . ?"

"You'd better come in," Dr. Samson said, eyeing the gawping crowd by the gate. Aveyard beckoned to Sergeant Bruton, who walked down the
path and into the house.

"This is Mr. Robinson," Dr. Samson said, "and
that was his wife."

"Was . . . ?"

"Sorry. I mean, is his wife. You'll have to
forgive me if I'm a little woolly; I've been up all
night with that corpse of yours!"

Stanley Robinson was fifty-six, but looked
seventy. He was dressed in a pair of trousers too
large about the waist, hanging from him on braces.
He had pulled on a shirt, but failed to tuck it in and
the tail flap was hanging. He hadn't brushed his
hair or put in his upper set of teeth. Sergeant Bruton
knew this wasn't the first time he'd seen Stanley
Robinson, though as yet the name or the face didn't
mean anything specific. Sergeant Bruton took him
into the sitting room.

"You were saying . . ." Aveyard prompted the
Doctor. His face was grey; he looked exhausted.

"I sent for you. Well, I phoned in, and they
told me you were out here somewhere working, and
they'd contact you. That woman's been poisoned,
and from the looks of her, she's had enough to kill
several people!"

## Other titles in the Walker British Mystery Series

JAMES
FRASER

# Death
in a
Pheasant's
Eye

WALKER AND COMPANY · NEW YORK

First published in the United States of America in 1972 by the Walker Publishing Company, Inc.

This paperback edition first published in 1984.

ISBN: 0-8027-3093-0

Library of Congress Catalog Card Number: 73-188474

Printed in the United States of America

10  9  8  7  6  5  4  3  2  1

*for*
*BRIAN SCARTH*
*MR and MRS COLLIS,*
*and JOHN AVEYARD*
*with thanks*

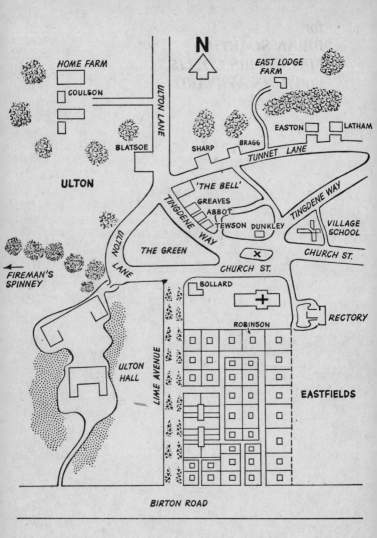

# FRIDAY EVENING, NOVEMBER FIFTH

Harry Greaves poured paraffin over the wood; when the can was nearly empty he jerked it upwards, trying to splash the effigy of Guy Fawkes at the top of the pyre. The liquid wouldn't reach that high. "Leave it, Harry," several impatient villagers said, "it'll burn!" He lighted four matches held together, gave them to Matthew Bragg who'd earned the right, and Matthew tossed them among the wood; the flames whipped round the perimeter then soared into the night sky.

The pyramid of flame shot upwards with the staccato crackle of machine gun fire; kids set rockets in tin cans and fathers insisted on being the one to light 'em; devil's beard flaring red spat globules of intense heat; Catherine wheels whirled on sticks; tiny kids held sparklers like haloes and ran into the dark; fiery snow and cascading moon fountain spurted incandescent, the brilliant aluminium light plucking village faces from the darkness. Women smiled warily clasping their purses in their hands; John Western looked anxiously at Julian, his guest, hoping he was enjoying the occasion. The flames reached up the four-by-four and engulfed the pyre and then, to everyone's surprise, the effigy of the Guy Fawkes fell into the holocaust below.

"That's dropped down a bit quick," Harry Greaves said, "it can't have been fastened properly!"

It was Julian, the American, who spotted it; as the effigy tumbled from its pole one leg of the trousers pulled out of the rubber boot, which had split with the heat. The rubber boot dropped into the heart of the fire where it started to flare.

Sticking from the end of the trousers' leg was, unmistakably, a human foot.

7

## CHAPTER TWO

Detective Superintendent Bill Aveyard was sitting in his flat near Birton wearing paint-stained levis and a grey woollen shirt that three months ago would have been thought modern. He was drinking a cup of coffee and wondering whether to cook supper or paint the inside of the living-room door.

"Damn all women!" he said. He'd been stood up!

Usually he worked week-ends to give time off to married colleagues; this week he'd been careful to check he was free except for emergencies. He'd had a date!

"What shall we do?" he asked the girl, a twenty-two years old brunette who attended Birton Tech. "Dinner somewhere, bottle of wine, back to my place to listen to records?" Hardly a subtle approach, but it hadn't failed him in the past.

That was when she surprised him. He knew she was a painter now working on pottery. "I've got something I'd like you to look at," she said.

"A piece of pottery you've made?"

"No!" she said, seeming embarrassed, "it's something I've never tried before. I'd like to know what you think. Can I bring them up to your place on Friday night. We could eat in."

"What are 'they'?"

"Etchings!" she said.

# CHAPTER THREE

The heat of the blaze prevented them getting near the pyre; it was too far to run a hose-pipe from the nearest house, Fred Dunkley's in Tingdene Way, but they managed as best they could with a chain of buckets.

When Harry Greaves finally got through to the emergency service on 999, they warned him it would be some time before a fire appliance could come. Six fires were burning in the County and one of them at a chemical factory threatened a housing estate and a hospital.

"We think there's a dead body ...!"

"In the fire ...? Blimey ...!"

"So we'd better have the police ..."

"I'll notify them. What's your telephone number?"

"Crowsfoot 209."

"You're not pulling my leg. I mean, you did say there's a dead body in the Bonfire on the Green at Ulton?"

"I'm not pulling your leg. I'm the village postmaster ..."

"Always something different on this job! Leave it with me ..."

The body would have remained on the fire if Arthur Tewson hadn't fetched a five prong draw hoe he tied to the end of a coil of wire. He flung it into the flames and grappled out the grisly charred remains, barely recognisable as a human cadaver.

Amy Dunkley, sensitive soul, fetched a sheet.

Tom Bollard, the blacksmith, and his son Aubrey, shooed away curious kids. Dodson Bragg, Arthur Tewson and Stan Coulson stood guard over the sheet, which was already running with water, sooted and charred at one corner. The Reverend Francis Elks knelt on the grass and composed a prayer, old Olive Abbott stonefaced beside him.

9

Bert Larrapin opened the pub, The Bell, on the corner of Tingdene Way and Tunnet Lane. It filled immediately with husbands *and* wives and Bert's wife Esther and his son William, had to go behind the bar to help him serve. There was only one subject of conversation.

"Who do you suppose it is? Man or woman?"

Everyone took a tally of his neighbours. "I haven't seen Benny Latham all day ..."

"He was at the Bonfire ..."

"Are you sure? I didn't see him ..."

"Richard Hopton ...?"

"Harrowing the Five Acre at teatime ..."

"Roger Blatsoe ... ?"

"Taking corn down the Spinney ..."

"Wasn't at the Bonfire ..."

"Wouldn't expect 'im, would you, a gamekeeper! He's never where the village can see 'im, is 'e, case somebody slips off and grabs 'is pheasants ..."

"But who do you suppose it could be?"

# CHAPTER FOUR

The telephone rang. Bill Aveyard set the paint brush on the side of the paint can, glanced at the clock. He picked up the telephone. "About time," he said.

"Is that Birton 297?"

"Yes, Superintendent Aveyard here." He recognised the voice of the police telephone operator. There were clicks on the line, then the familiar voice of the Detective Chief Superintendent, like wet gravel on corrugated iron, growled into his ear.

"Aveyard ...?"

"Yes, Chief ...?"

"How's your stomach?"

"Empty, Chief!"

"Keep it that way, and get out to Ulton. Bonfire on the Green ..."

"I thought we agreed, Chief, that I was off duty tonight except for emergencies ..."

"They were using a human being as the Guy!" The phone clicked dead.

When Aveyard arrived at Ulton village, ten minutes later, all the official wheels had been set in efficient motion. He looked around the Green for his Sergeant, smiled when he saw Bruton had not yet arrived. Three police cars, and eight policemen, traffic routed along the north side of Church Street and Tingdene Way, and south along the face of the Church. Good. The Bonfire had been lit on a small patch of ground to the east of the larger triangular village Green, almost directly in front of the Church. Though it had finally been extinguished, plumes of smoke and steam rose from its remains. The white sheet covered the corpse, and three men stood nearby. Good. Aveyard climbed from his car, still wearing denims and

11

the grey woollen shirt, and walked to where the patrol car Sergeant was standing guard near the sheet.

The Sergeant recognising him instantly, saluted him in the way of an older man. Aveyard was the youngest Detective Superintendent on the Birton Force, and few of the old hands would forget it.

Aveyard stood by the sheet. "Forensic?" he asked.

"On the way, Superintendent. Want to look?"

Aveyard shook his head. "There'll be time for that when the pathologist gets here."

The Sergeant nodded gravely.

"Sergeant Bruton?"

"On his way. He's stopped to pick up the Doctor."

"Who's on tonight, Samson?"

"He was supposed to be off, but everybody else's busy ..."

"I was painting a door ..."

"I've had the trots all day! I was thinking of reporting sick ..."

"Find yourself a cork ...?"

"Something like that!"

"I hate Bonfire Night."

"Don't we all?"

Sergeant arrived two minutes later, with Doctor Samson, the police surgeon. The official team arrived at the same time, stood surveying the Bonfire site and the surrounding ground. The police photographer snapped a plate into his camera, but stood there bemused. "What a bastard!" he said. "Where shall I start?" Rules for police photographers said, 'take a shot of the scene of the crime showing the setting and position of the corpse'. But what was the setting? A smoking, steaming pile of half burned rubbish that had been doused with water and kicked about, surrounded by a grass strip on which every blessed foot in the village had walked. He adjusted the flash mechanism, set aperture and exposure, held the camera to his eye and squeezed the trigger.

Doctor Samson and Sergeant Bruton grasped the top corners of the sheet, lifted it aside and placed it on the ground. The Doctor stood on the sheet, placed his bag beside the cadaver and squatted. The photographer held the camera to his eye and pressed the trigger, recording the position and appearance of the corpse.

The Doctor held his knees with his hands and looked. There was nothing he could do. Bruton walked to Aveyard standing ten feet away, looking at nothing, seeing everything.

"Bad luck, Jim," Bill Aveyard said. They'd worked together on many cases, knew each other well enough to share a moment's informality before getting on with the job. "Who has Ulton these days?"

"Nobody, Superintendent. They closed the police house last week when Constable Fellowes died."

"Old Syd, dead; I didn't know that. What did he die of ...?"

"We all think it was cancer, but they're not saying ... Anyway, they've amalgamated Ulton with Little Borrowden. It was in this week's orders ..."

"Paperwork! Pity, Old Syd could have told us the ins and outs ..."

Doctor Samson completed his preliminary examination then stood up, and Aveyard walked quickly forward.

"Nothing else I can do here," the Doctor said, "you've notified the pathologist?"

"Yes, he's on his way ..."

"I'll start writing up my notes for him. This is one time I'm glad they moved the body!"

"Sit in my car," Aveyard said, "it's warmer in there."

"You ought to have a coat on, a night like this ..."

"I've got a duffle coat in the car when I need it!"

Aveyard didn't feel the cold, yet, though the night was bitter. Smoke rose from the smouldering pyre, but all the heat had been doused by the buckets of water. Many of the villagers had eyes rimmed with smoke from their fire-quenching efforts. As the Doctor got into the car, a fire tender drove up with its light flashing and two note siren screaming. The fire officer ran across to Aveyard.

"It's out," Aveyard said.

"We were at a chemical factory fire in Brought ..."

"It's all go tonight!"

"Damn Bonfire Night! I'm always on duty, but it wouldn't make any difference ..."

"All hands to the pumps, eh ...?"

"Thank God for a sense of humour, Superintendent ...!"

"We'll both need it!"

Aveyard shivered, accepted his duffle coat gratefully when Bruton brought it from the car. "Can't have the general public thinking you're a hippie, Superintendent," Bruton said.

## CHAPTER FIVE

Ulton village is twenty minutes bus ride from Birton on high ground overlooking the valley of the River Nene. Ulton Church is one of many in that part of the world built by the stonemasons from Stamford who delighted in spires and, legend has it, women and ale. The Ulton spire appears slightly crooked if you look at it from the Birton Road and local wags who served in Italy with the County Regiment have nicknamed it 'The Pisa of Northamptonshire', a bit of an extravagance since the tilt is no more than a half of one degree. A clue to the tilt was discovered in 1969 when stonemasons climbed the spire to effect a small repair, and found a couple of old bottles, sloping down at the shoulder, built into the back of the stone, doubtless depriving one of the original stonemasons but ensuring his sobriety at those tricky heights.

Before the Birton Road was widened at that point, the Church was presented to the eye at the far end of a field whose only occupants were pheasants, foxes, and Ulton courting couples. It was an idyllic setting, especially on an autumn evening when the trees blazed red and purple and brown. Dodson Bragg's shiftless dear departed father owned fifty acres of that land but when his fecklessness and the Labour Government's restrictions finally overcame him in the late sixties, he sold out to Johnny Mann, who'd made a bob or two pushing a cart full of black market stuff when the other men of the village were trying to yank the Germans off Monte Cassino.

Johnny Mann's pals on the County Council had shared many a doubtful deal with him in the past, and they saw to it he obtained planning permission for building. Nowadays when you come up the hill from Kettering towards Ulton, the reds and browns and purples have gone, and grey concrete and

15

bright red brick suppurate over the landscape like some fearful skin disease. Mann Close, Mann Avenue, Mann Way and Terrace, Mann Crescent, Lane and Road; Johnny Mann left his name behind like the stonemasons of old left empty bottles, bastards and spires; now he lives over at Broxworth where he's pulling down the fourteenth-century Tithe Barn to build a supermarket; he's driven everywhere in a white Jaguar that looks too big even for him; he has ulcers and dyspepsia, and his wife has run away with a waiter. Only the postman and the electoral rolls observe the Mann addresses. The rest of the village, old when ink was wet on the Domesday Book, still calls the new estate Eastfields as it has since time immemorial. Johnny Mann's greatest crime, however, was to lay an axe to the avenue of limes along which people walk from the bus-stop in Birton Road. That avenue of limes stretches alongside the wall that has shielded Ulton Hall for over five hundred years. John Western earned his seat on the parish council by getting a lawyer from Birton to nail a preservation order on the Lime Avenue the minute Johnny Mann started lopping. Now it's officially scheduled as being 'Of Historic Interest', and there's nothing any man breathing can do about it.

Ulton Lane branches left and right when it comes to the village Green. On the left it curves round the Green, straightens again, and carries on past Home Farm which the Coulsons have rented for a couple of hundred years. On the right branch, Ulton Lane becomes Church Street since it passes along the north face of the Church itself. On the top side of the Green, north east, is Tingdene Way; the pub known as The Bell since it was once owned by a retired ship's captain who installed his old ship's bell in the yard some three hundred years ago, is at the top corner where Tingdene Way joins the continuation of Ulton Lane and Tunnet Lane. The village shop on Tingdene Way, overlooking the village Green, is kept by Harry Greaves, a bachelor of fifty. Next door, only a sparrow-spit, is the stone-built cottage where Olive Abbott lives; in a large window at street level hangs a white wedding dress and a once purple velvet costume and a purple dyed straw hat that Olive sewed as a going-away outfit for her honeymoon in Skegness with Samuel Abbott 'as was killed in the First World War'. The

Curator of Northampton Folk Museum has kept his eye on that dress for twenty years, and even bought moth balls out of his own pocket; Olive has promised it for display when she's 'dead and gone'. Students from the Royal College of Needlework once organised a coach tour to look at the dress, in which it's been estimated Olive sewed no less than fifty thousand stitches more accurate than the tapestries that hang in the Clothworkers Court in London. Olive's ancestors used to make lace in that cottage; she was born with nimble fingers.

Next door to Olive lives Arthur Tewson, aged sixty-one, and his son Sam Tewson who's sixteen and whose mother died giving birth to him too late in life. Sam works for Stan Coulson on Home Farm but his claim to fame is an ancestor, a servant to Thomas à Becket when he stood trial at Northampton Castle. In Tewson's front cupboard, wrapped in yellowed tissue paper in a tin box made for Queen Victoria's Coronation, is an old iron locket once said to contain a wisp of Thomas à Becket's hair culled when the servant was preparing his master for trial. Now the locket contains a pinch of snuff-like dust which Sam wants to send to Northampton for analysis; his Dad won't permit such sacrilege. Never mind, Dad can't last for ever and the locket becomes Sam's inheritance in twenty or thirty years time to do with as he will.

"That's the modern way," his Dad says whenever he catches Sam looking in the locket, "you young 'uns take nothing on trust. You have to question everything, smear your doubts on everything. In my day we were willing to believe ..." Can winter talk to spring?

The Reverend Francis Elks has moved the altar of Ulton Church into the nave. Now the chancel is used as a Lady Chapel. All the pews at the sides and back of the Church have been taken out; a number of black fibre-glass chairs are littered casually round the fourteenth-century font, and the Mothers' Union holds coffee mornings there. He even serves coffee after Sunday Evensong, and secular chat. The old hands distrust these innovations of course, but Francis Elks thinks they'll come round to his way of thinking, especially since he provides ginger nuts with the coffee and there's nothing Stan Coulson, vicar's warden and patriarch of the faithful of the village, likes better than a ginger nut.

The Reverend Francis Elks and his wife Jo walked back towards the Rectory on the east side of the Church. They didn't speak. From time to time Jo glanced at her husband as they walked up the Rectory drive, guessing his mood. Francis didn't like death, had never been able to regard it as a happy release. He also abhorred violence, and for the body to be placed at the stake like that implied violence in the manner of death. She reached out and touched his hand; his opened and clasped hers and they walked together up the drive. On the left was the gate of the Rectory, on the right the side gate of the Church yard.

Suddenly, Francis stopped. "What's that?" he said quietly.

Jo looked about her. She'd heard nothing except, perhaps, the rustle of the parkin tray against the tweed of her winter skirt. "I didn't hear anything," she said.

"Listen!"

She heard a scuffling in the Church yard.

Francis swung the Church yard gate open, its hinges screeching viciously. A figure charged towards them through the gloom, banged savagely into her, and sent the parkin tray to the stones with an unholy clatter. Francis grabbed at a shoulder but the small figure squirmed from his grasp, scuttled through the gateway and up the alley.

"Are you all right?"

She picked up the tray. "Yes, I'm all right. Who was it?"

"Bert Dunkley," Francis said, "I'd know that young lad anywhere." He ran up the path towards the Church and round the south side, towards Eastfields and the Church wall. A ladder, left on the ground by workmen pointing the stonework high under the eaves of the choir room, had been lifted against the choir-room wall. At the bottom of the ladder lay a coil of lead taken from the roof. Francis climbed the ladder quickly. Only one section of lead appeared to have been removed.

"They must have expected me to stay later at the Bonfire," he said when he came down. He pulled the cord that lowered the top section of the ladder, dragged it away from the wall to let it fall on the ground.

Fred and Amy Dunkley lived on the other side of the Bonfire site, almost opposite the Church. The Rector knocked on the door, which Amy opened wide. They went inside. In the centre of the room on a sofa, Olive Abbott sat drinking a cup of Bovril. "The sight at the Bonfire seems to have upset her," Fred Dunkley said. "We've offered her the spare bed but she won't stay the night."

"I like my own bed!" Olive said. She hadn't spent a night away from home since she returned from her honeymoon.

"I'll walk to the cottage with you when you've had a bit of a rest," Amy volunteered. She turned to the Rector. "What a terrible affair this is," she said, "would you like a cup of tea ...?"

"Join me in something a bit stronger," Fred offered, indicating the whisky bottle he'd been saving for Christmas. The Rector standing inside the door, Jo squashed beside him, cleared his throat.

"It's a sad affair at the Bonfire," he said, "but I'm afraid that's not why we've come to see you." His manner apologetic he looked at Olive then said, "I'm afraid it's something more personal ..."

"About Bert ..." Jo added. The Rector looked disapproving at her. As soon as Jo mentioned Bert's name, Olive looked up at them, fully alert. "What's my poor little Bert been up to?" she asked. "He come in her like the devil was chasing 'im. Not you, was it?"

"I'm afraid it was!"

"What can the poor little mite possibly have done ...?"

Fred and Amy glanced at each other in exasperation. Ever since Bert had been born, Olive had taken a strong personal interest in him. She'd sewn an entire layette for the baby, all stitched with meticulous care, so beautiful Amy had not had the heart to refuse it. Every year she provided the young child with new clothes, gave presents for his birthday, invited him into her cottage and fed him. Fred tried to stop her, but Amy always excused her. "She must be very lonely," she'd said, "losing her only boy in the last war. If our Bert's a bit company for her, well why not ..."

"What's the lad been doing this time?" Fred said.

19

"This time, this time, there you go again," Olive screeched. "Judging him in advance ..."

"I'm afraid there's no doubt this time," Francis Elks said. "While we were at the Bonfire there must have been a gang. I suppose it's the Eastfields lot. They put a ladder behind the Church and stripped a course of lead from the roof of the choir room. There must have been at least three to carry down the lead. I suppose we got back earlier than they anticipated, and Bert panicked. Almost knocked Mrs Elks over dashing past us. I'm afraid I recognised his face. I'm sorry!"

Even Olive was silent. Fred's face mottled with anger. He strode to the door at the foot of the bedroom stairs, opened it, and bellowed up. "Come down here, you little bugger!"

Amy standing beside Olive clutched her shoulders.

"You won't hurt him, Fred, will you," she pleaded. He'd unbuckled the two inch wide leather belt he wore round his waist; he rolled it and put it in a drawer, lest he should use it in anger. As soon as the boy appeared he reached up the stairs, grabbed him, and dragged him down into the sitting room. The boy had gone to bed wearing his shirt and underpants. He stood trembling in front of Fred, looking down at the carpet. Fred put his hand on the boy's shoulder.

"Been stealing lead, you little bugger?" he said. It wasn't a question; the boy's guilt was quite apparent.

Francis Elks looked at his wife. He could see she was terrified; with no children of her own she was tender towards all young people.

"Were you stealing the lead from the roof of the choir room?" Francis asked, his voice quiet. The boy nodded. His father gripped his shoulder. "Speak when you're spoken to!" he said, his voice trembling with quiet anger. Olive started to whimper and Amy comforted her.

"Yes," the boy said.

Fred thrust Bert from him. "That a lad of ours should do a thing like that ..." he said. "Right, give us the names. We want the full names of everybody there. Then it's the police for you, my lad." Amy started to wail, pulling up the hem of her pinny to cover her face. The boy looked at Fred unable to believe what he had heard.

"I forgave you when you was stealing from the shop, I forgave you again when you nicked a pound out of your mother's purse ..."

"You bashed me both times!" the boy said, and reeled back when Fred's leg-of-mutton hand smashed against the side of his face.

The Rector stepped forward, held Fred's arm. "Don't hit him," he pleaded. "I think we can settle the matter between us!"

Fred turned to him, his face dulled with disappointment. "I'm sorry, Rector, but it's gone too far this time. The lad's got a streak of the devil in him! I'm afraid it's up to the police. Slip up to the Square, Amy, and fetch a bobby." Amy looked at him for a moment, tears in her eyes. "I'm sorry, love," he said, tenderly, "but this time I mean it ..."

There was a look between them no other could have comprehended. Amy and Fred Dunkley had been married twenty two years, and during the first eleven years of their life together had remained childless. Eleven years ago, on her way back from East Lodge Farm late at night, Amy had been attacked just off Tunnet Lane and raped. The assailant had never been discovered. Nine months later she gave birth to Bert. Fred and she never had another child and though everyone accepted Bert as Fred's son and the rape was forgotten, in their hearts both knew the truth. Whoever Bert's father had been, some part of his personality was stamped on the child indelible as the mark of Cain.

"It's for the boy's own good," Fred said, softly.

Amy wiped her face on the pinny and went from the cottage. All were silent as the door shut behind her, then Olive, sitting on the sofa, cackled. "Sacrilege, that's what you've done my boy," she said, "they'll put you away!"

The Rector looked at his wife then both crossed the room to the sofa. "Come on, Olive," Jo said, "we'll take you home."

"I imagine the police will want me for identification," the Rector said, "but I'd rather not wait here for them if you don't mind. Anyway, they'll need me to show them the ladder and the lead."

"I've got to go to the lavat'ry!" Bert suddenly wailed.

# CHAPTER SIX

The routine investigation had begun and Sergeant Bruton checked the names of everyone at the Bonfire against the copy of the electoral roll Harry Greaves supplied. Two hundred people lived in Ulton; the Sergeant's mathematical mind saw that unusually, there were more males than females, and a family average of only two children. Harry Greaves knew everyone; he supplied ages, and potted biographies; even remembered John and Jeanne Western and the American who didn't appear on the roll. He explained the shortage of children.

"The folks in the village are too old for young kids, except Stephany Latham with her four and there's no stopping her. The Eastfields lot are mostly newlyweds. That's where Johnny Mann was clever; he picked names from engagement lists in the local paper and offered hundred per cent mortgages. Some of 'em moved in before the plaster was dry! They're all about due over there; soon there'll be more big bellies than hot dinners ..."

Dodson Bragg and Arthur Tewson stood by to jog his memory; in less than half an hour the Sergeant knew something about all the folks of the village.

"Was there anything at all unusual about this year's Bonfire?" he asked several times. Policemen are trained to look for breaks in pattern and habit, out-of-the-ordinary events that other people miss. Each time he received the same answer; the only thing unusual was the presence of a stranger.

"You understand, Sergeant," Dodson Bragg said, "we have an order of doing things in a village. Everything, you might say, has a ritual of simple things a town-bred person wouldn't understand. For example, the kids always come first to the Bonfire; they go home from school, get washed, and gather

22

about five o'clock round the pile of wood, tidying it you might say, throwing everything onto the pyramid in a neat pile. But in reality they're judging a competition. 'I brought that plank; he brought that settee; one settee's worth five planks; Willie brought that chair, and that's worth say three planks ...' By about a quarter to six they'd decided among themselves who's the King of the Bonfire, who's provided the most stuff. He's the one gets the honour of throwing the match. Like I said, it's a ritual. The first adult to come down is Stan Coulson. Don't ask me why, it's always been the tenant of Home Farm. Stan Coulson always wears a hat on Bonfire Night, never on any other day of the year even for funerals. The rest of us look out for him in that hat, and nobody'd think of leaving their house before that hat appeared. Take the matter of the paraffin. Henry, here, took that over when he bought the business; if he hadn't honoured that tradition all these years, he'd never sell so much as an ice cream over his counter!"

"Blackmail, that's what *that* is!" Harry said, smiling.

"The last person to arrive is always whoever occupies the Hall. At the moment it's Arthur Newsome, young Mr Arthur as we still call him though he's going on fifty-two. We don't know who'll carry on after him since he's never married and has no heirs. At least, so far as we know he has none, though he was a bit of a rip in his time!" He chuckled at the memory. "They used to tell one story, well, it's a bit of a sidetrack ..."

"Go on," the Sergeant said, "I like a story ..."

"Well, nobbut gossip really, but they do say when he was in full pride out hunting he'd lift the girl of his choice off her horse and onto his, sit her in his lap, and down wi' her jodhpurs at full gallop!" He chuckled again. "Story came out when the very Honourable Ellie Fitzbarton had to have quickthorns extracted from her bare arse. The horse chose a tactless moment to jump a six-foot hedge ...!"

"Liked his oats, our young Mr Arthur did ..." Arthur Tewson said, as they all laughed at the story, "but there *is* one thing was different this year, if the Sergeant's interested in details ...?"

The Sergeant was avid for details.

"That Guy. Something different about that ..." Arthur

Tewson looked round the group, proud of himself, challenging anyone to match his memory. Each one thought, but no-one could recall anything significant.

"That Guy usually stays up 'til the four by four's burned. This year it dropped, hardly before the fire got started. Bloody hot that fire gets in the heart. If the Guy had been held there with *wire*, according to tradition, there'd 'a been nothing left for you to ask questions about ...!"

Sergeant Bruton had turned over a page. 'Tied with rope, not wire,' he wrote, then 'why?' "Who helped the boys fasten the Guy?" he asked Harry Greaves.

"Benny Latham. Husband of Stephany as has all the kids. About forty-nine. Lives in Tunnet Lane and works on and off for Bill Hopton of East Lodge Farm. You lads have had him in a time or two ... Only telling you now because you're bound to find out. Benny Latham's what you might call the blot on our village escutcheon!"

"Tying that Guy wi' rope instead of wire; Benny will never live that down," Dodson Bragg said, shaking his head.

"If Benny was the last person to tie it ..." the Sergeant said.

Detective Superintendent Aveyard was standing by the remains of the pyre; Sergeant Bruton walked across to him.

"This all has to be raked over carefully and sifted," Aveyard said.

"What are we looking for?" Sergeant Bruton asked.

"How should I know? You understand the drill as well as I do. Anything that shouldn't be there, anything odd, though I'd take a bet right now we shan't find a thing and wind up like the Black and White Minstrels ..." Aveyard was rattled, and that took a lot of doing. Bruton had been on many cases with him, but had never seen him like this. Usually, Aveyard approached a case with quiet enthusiasm, like an addict who's just received a new book of crossword puzzles.

"We might pay special attention to any *wire* we find ..."

"You on to something, Sergeant?"

"The Guy was usually tied to the post with wire. Whoever re-tied it with the corpse inside must have used rope according to a report I've just had." They were standing together, looking at the smouldering remains as if praying a voice could

24

speak from the ashes when Amy Dunkley approached them.

"Would you be Detective Superintendent Aveyard?" she asked.

"I would, ma'am. What can I do for you?"

"An ordinary bobby would do but they told me to ask for you ..." she said, eyeing his paint-spattered jeans and his duffle coat, disarmed by his obvious youth.

He nodded. Nobody ever believed it, first time. If only he had a pound for every time somebody had said, 'My, aren't you young'. Sometimes he felt ninety-five years old, like now!

"It's about my boy ... My husband wondered ... could you spare a minute?"

"What about your boy? Anything to do with this fire?" Sergeant Bruton heard the quickening interest in Aveyard's voice. The truculence had vanished. Now Aveyard was all policeman.

"What's your name missis?" Bruton asked, then identified Amy Dunkley from the electoral roll. "Your boy, that'd be Bert, I take it ...?"

"We can get the details later," Aveyard said with some asperity. "What *about* your boy Bert ...?"

"I'd rather leave that to my husband, if you don't mind," Amy said, tears filling her eyes. Bruton glanced at the address on the rolls. "It's quite near," he said, "and while we're waiting for forensic ..." They set off walking after Amy Dunkley, who'd run from the scene of the Bonfire across Tingdene Way into the gate of the cottage. Bruton noted the tiny but immaculate garden, newly-painted window frames, thatch recently re-wired. Mental note: occupants careful, tidy, homeloving. Aveyard was looking at the door which opened as Amy approached it, and the man who loomed large there, trousers hanging below his stomach. 'Forty-five,' Aveyard thought automatically, 'farm worker or such, strong, not too bright, loves his wife ...' then speculation ended as the man opened the door wide to let them in.

"This is the Superintendent in charge," Amy said. The man nodded without speaking, standing aside to let them enter, then walked to the foot of the bedroom stairs in the entrance room. They didn't waste space on 'halls' when they built these

25

cottages; halls came later with Victorian pretension. Door left is probably a parlour seldom used; a Spider plant in the window, green velvet or brown cover on the table, a china cabinet containing a few well polished figures an auctioneer'd give his back teeth to put under the hammer, since they came down from grannie's gran who bought 'em when Josiah Wedgwood first started, trundling his own hand-cart.

"Bert!" the man shouted. "Come down here!" Careful voice, but firm. Country timbre with the careful enunciation of a patient man. Bruton's finger was on the electoral roll showing a name to Aveyard. Names, dates, places, fish and chips to the Sergeant, staff of life. "Would you be Fred Dunkley?" the Sergeant asked, seeking to put things on a proper footing. "Yes, that's me," Fred said without turning his head. "Bert, come down here at once!" he shouted up the steps. There was no reply. Fred turned to Amy. "He went out to the lavatory. When I saw you coming, I went to fetch him in, but he wasn't there. I thought he must have slipped upstairs ..."

They searched the house, the back garden, the outside lavatory, but could find no trace of Bert.

Amy wailed when they realised he was missing. "He hasn't even got his trousers on ..." she cried.

# CHAPTER SEVEN

It was dark in the village when Aveyard and Bruton walked together up Tunnet Lane, a cold November night. The trees on either side of the lane stripped of foliage rustled in a light wind, branches rubbing on branches in an endless and macabre whisper. East Lodge Farm on the left behind a carefully brushed hawthorn hedge split, bent, and laid in old fashioned style to fortify the boundary. Lights shone from a couple of the cottages down the lane that led back into Tingdene Way, but ahead of them all was darkness. Tunnet Lane had no pavement, and they walked in the centre of the once asphalted road, away from the hedges.

"Was that an owl?" Sergeant Bruton asked, shivering despite his heavy tweed overcoat. Coppers are not supposed to be afraid of the dark.

"Don't ask *me* ..."

One cottage on the left. All dark. Front garden's overgrown; line of Brussels sprouts down the left of the path, waiting for the snows to make 'em tasty. A plain grey mini-van parked in a lean-to garage, a kid's bike on the path. "Damn," Sergeant Bruton muttered, catching his leg. Front door hidden in a small portico that has two seats, both littered with kids' toys, plastic ducks, a pair of tin scales used for playing shops. No knocker. No bell either.

A dog started to bark, somewhere inside, feet scampering on bare lino, scratching, shouting his head off.

Aveyard stood beneath the portico in shadow. Bruton was in shadow, but at the side of the house where he could watch the back. A policeman's knock has a way of advertising its origin and many a man slips out of the back when he hears one at the front. Aveyard pounded the door, once, twice, three

27

times. A knock's a knock, isn't it, but how come his knock on this old oak door should sound solemn as the proverbial knell of doom. The dog shut up, in mid-bark. No sound from within, no sound. Aveyard stepped back, looked up at the roughly curtained bedroom windows. Whatever else Stephany Latham may be good at, she's no good at sewing to judge by the curtains and the holes in 'em. Take your time before you knock again. Give a man a chance to get out of bed, pull on his pants, and walk down the stairs.

Aveyard lifted his hand to knock again.

A voice spoke from the hedge on his right. "Who is it?" Aveyard turned. This side of the hedge was in deep shadow. "Who is it?" the voice asked again. Aveyard glanced towards his Sergeant, invisible to his eye in the shadow of the wall.

"What you after, the pair of you?" the voice said. He could see them both.

"If that's Benny Latham," Aveyard said, "we've come to ask you about that Guy you fixed on the Bonfire ..."

"And what else?"

"Nothing else, at the moment!"

Benny Latham stepped from the shadow of the hedge, a shotgun cradled beneath his arm, the dog silent by his side. As he walked forward the dog walked with him, nose level with his calf. He dropped his hand. The dog sat, instantly. They could see him quite clearly now in the moon's bright light.

"What do you want to know?" Benny asked.

"You got a licence for that gun?" Bruton asked, coming to stand by Aveyard.

Benny ignored him. "What do you want to know about the Bonfire?" he said to Aveyard. Aveyard put his hand on the Sergeant's arm. Questions about the gun could come later. "They say you were the one helped the kids tie the Guy to the stake ...?"

"They'd say anything about a Latham."

Pause. No more coming. This isn't a man to volunteer information. Five feet ten and a half inches, give or take a quarter of an inch. Weight, approximately thirteen stone seven, and none of it fat. Rough face, rough hands, rough manner. His nose has been broken sometime, smashed probably

28

by the heel of the hand of someone rough as he is. A hundred years ago he'd have been the village prize-fighter, if they could ever have taught him the rules. That dog's part of him. Try to get near him and the dog'll bite a lump out of your calf, but let a kid tickle it and it'd roll on its back like an idiot.

"Did you tie the Guy to the stake?" Stay with straight questions and you'll get answers.

"Is that a crime these days?"

"It's no crime," Aveyard said wearily. Why did it always have to be like this? A policeman can't work without help, but why were the Benny Lathams of this world always so suspicious? "I wouldn't even bother you except I think you may be able to help us with our enquiries ..."

Benny Latham smiled, a bitter grimace. "I've heard that before," he said. Aveyard could have bitten out his tongue. It was the stock phrase they use when they hold a man without arrest. Everyone in the country knows that 'helping with our enquiries' can mean 'we're holding somebody, and we'll arrest him properly when we have enough evidence against him'.

"I don't mean it that way. We're not going to ask you to come down to the station. I merely want to ask you about the way you tied the Guy to the stake."

"Bloody persecution, that's what this is, coming round here in the middle of the night."

"How did you tie it? What kind of knot did you use?"

"Are you bloody crazy or something. How the hell should I remember what kind of knots I used. There were these two kids with the Guy. I was going to Harry Greaves to buy a smoke, and they asked me to give 'em a bit of a hand. Fancy them, asking a Latham to help 'em! Anyway, I give 'em a lift wi' it, up onto the Bonfire, and then lashed the Guy to the stake."

"What with?" Take it steady. Don't lead him. Let him tell you he used wire, or rope. People don't remember simple things, but if you plant an idea in their minds they'll swear blue murder that's what happened. "What did you tie it with?"

"I dunno. I tied it, isn't that enough? How do I know what

29

with? A bit of string, a piece of rope, wire, anything."

"Benny, it's very important for us to know what you tied it with, and how you tied it."

Benny's mind was racing. They were after something. That bloody man, standing back a bit, had the smell of a long-time Sergeant, a collar grabber, about him. Now that Syd Fellowes had gone, Benny had been hoping for a bit of peace, but that Sergeant had a look of iron hands. What were they after? How did he tie the Guy to the Bonfire?—well, that was a load of old cobblers, wasn't it? Whatever he told them they'd say— 'Oh, used string did you, and *where did you get the string?*' or 'used wire, eh?— well, Coulson up at Home Farm has just reported the loss of a bale of peat bound with wire!'. He'd had a bale of peat instead of wages but how could he prove it? His chrysanths would suffer without it and they were worth fifteen pence a pot to him in the shops at Christmas. He'd paid good money for a coil of string in Harry Greaves, but who ever asks for a receipt? He'd *found* a rope, well he'd found a tarpaulin with it, hadn't he, off a lorry but who was he to say where it had come from? What were these buggers looking for? Ten to one there was a catch in it, somewhere. As usual, they were out to trip him; it was allus the same! "There was a piece of chain on one of the posts in the Bonfire. I fixed the Guy wi' that, on account of I didn't have no rope nor wire. That's what I fixed the Guy wi', a bit of an old chain I found on a post thrown out for the Bonfire!"

"You're absolutely certain?"

"Abso-bloody-lutely positive. Now can I tak the dog in? It's past his bed-time!"

"Just one or two more questions. That Guy, describe it for us, will you?"

"What is there to describe? It was a Guy. I saw the Bragg kids struggling with it and gave 'em a hand. We allus have a good Guy in Ulton, logs in it makes it burn better. It was too heavy for them to manage on their own ..."

"How heavy ..."

"How the hell do I know? I didn't weigh the bloody thing Picking on me ..."

Aveyard clenched his hands. "It's too late at night, Benny,

for playing games," he said. "Just answer the questions and we'll all get home to bed. Give me an estimate of how heavy the Guy was, and don't argue with me all the time."

"It weighed a bloody ton, I can tell you that!"

Aveyard shook his head. "It can't have weighed a ton, Benny, or the three of you together couldn't have lifted it. Did it weigh as much as, shall we say, a hundredweight bag of cement ..."

"Bag o' barley, more like ..." Latham said.

Aveyard looked at the Sergeant, mystified.

"A hundredweight and a half, or twelve stone, or a hundred and sixty eight pounds," Sergeant Bruton said, smiling. The Superintendent was too young for old fashioned rural weights and measures.

"What was in the Guy to weigh that much?"

"Straw, logs, bits of old rags, sticks to keep it straight. God knows what Olive puts in the Guys, but like I said, she allus stuffs 'em well, almost life-like ..."

"Could it have been a human body ...?" Aveyard asked.

So this was what they were after, eh? They'd have him for murder if he didn't watch out. "See here," Benny said, "you can't do me for what was in that Guy. So far as I knew, it was a Guy for the Bonfire. It weighed bloody 'eavy, and I damned near cricked my back gettin' it up there. How them two lads got it on the barrow I'll never know. But it was a Guy for the Bonfire, far as I was concerned, and you can't tell me different!"

"Nobody's saying you knew what was in it. But you handled it, and we want your impressions. Could it have been a human body inside? *Could* it have been?"

"It was straw, and logs, and old rags. There was straw sticking out of it, I tell you."

"And no human body, or nothing that felt like one?"

"How the hell should I know? I got the feel of it when I lifted it up. It felt like straw inside the clothes. Old Olive sewed it up well, and the trousers and the jacket stayed together, so I couldn't see right through it, but I'm telling you, it was straw and logs and old rags ..."

"Did it bend?" the Sergeant asked, thinking of rigor mortis.

31

If a corpse had been inside it, the corpse would have been stiff.

"No, it didn't bend, but it wasn't made to, was it. It was made to stand up there at the top of the Bonfire. Use your brains, Sergeant, who wants a Guy that flops down the minute you light the fire. Look, I'm not saying any more. So far as I knew, that was a Guy made of straw and logs and old rags I put on the Bonfire, not a stiff, and I'm not saying any more."

"You got a licence for that shotgun?" the Sergeant asked him, all official.

"It belongs to Richard Hopton. I was cleaning it."

"At this time of night. Don't you know it's an offence to carry a weapon, especially after dark?" Sergeant Bruton had a hatred of 'old lags' and recognised Benny Latham instantly as one of the breed.

Aveyard tapped the Sergeant's arm. "Somebody else can come and look at his shotgun licence," he said, "and while they're about it, they can look at the receipts for the timber and glass for that greenhouse he's built, and the brick base it's standing on. And they can check the licence and the insurance of that mini-van. I can't see Mr Latham wasting his money on things like that ..."

"Let 'em check all they want, Superintendent!" Benny Latham said. "They'll find me here! And if I'd known there was a stiff inside that Guy, I wouldn't have touched it for a pension!"

Neither of the Bragg children, woken from sleep, could remember how Latham had tied the Guy to the stake. "We left 'im to it," they explained. "We'd seen a chair Mr Larrapin had put outside the back door of the pub."

"Did you see a piece of fencing with a chain on it?"

"On the pile?"

"Yes."

"Could have been. We didn't notice it special, but there was lots of stuff like that."

They were dropping with sleep. Sylvia Bragg looked anxiously at them. She hadn't wanted them woken. "Can't it wait

32

until morning?" she'd asked Dodson Bragg, but he'd appointed himself special constable and wanted to help with their enquiries.

# CHAPTER EIGHT

Nobody had seen anything of any significance, of course, but who can tell what is significant and what isn't, except a trained policeman. Everybody Aveyard and Bruton questioned had walked past the Guy many times. The Guy was always made by Olive Abbott, had been, so far as anyone could remember, for fifty years or more. Olive was the village seamstress; nothing she couldn't manage with a needle and thread. She'd earned her living at it since her husband was killed at Mons leaving her pregnant from his last leave. Dodson Bragg's kids had gone as usual to collect the Guy from Olive's cottage in Tingdene Way. As usual, the Guy was ready for them, lying stretched out just inside the door, where it always was. Made a good Guy, did old Olive. The trousers, coat, shirt, balaclava helmet, and rubber boots all came from junk Sylvia Bragg kept in a shed behind the cottage in Tunnet Lane, since she could never bring herself to destroy anything and you could never tell, she explained, when something might be needed for a village Sale of Work. It was junk; the rubber boots were split at the heel, the jacket worn through at the elbows and patched time and again. The balaclava helmet had belonged to her Dad, knitted for him during the last war by her Mother, God rest her soul.

Simon and Matthew had taken the Guy to the site of the Bonfire on a flat cart; they tried to manhandle it onto the pile but couldn't manage on their own. It weighed too much. Benny Latham was passing at the time; they didn't want to ask him, well, it wasn't much good asking a Latham for anything, but he was the only one about. He helped 'em. They left him tying the Guy to the post.

The Guy had been in full view for two weeks; everyone in

the village saw it, everyone commented on it and what a splendidly life-like guy it was, but nobody could suggest how straw came to be transmuted into flesh; how a logs-and-rag effigy however well stuffed could turn itself into the remains of a human being.

Sergeant Bruton and Detective Superintendent Aveyard returned to Aveyard's flat during the night. "Mind the door," Aveyard said, "the paint's wet."

The Sergeant preferred tea to coffee.

Aveyard made a corned beef sandwich, sat down on the chair at the table in the living room to eat it. The Sergeant was sitting on the sofa, looking round the room.

"You're getting this place to look nice," he said, "it's marvellous what a coat o' paint'll do!" Neither one of them was thinking of paint at that moment.

"This is going to be a tough one," Bill Aveyard said.

The Sergeant nodded. He flicked open the pad in which he'd recorded details of the interviews they had conducted. His handwriting was meticulous but told him nothing. "Maybe the forensic boys'll pick up something?"

"They'll tell us whether it was a male or female; find the cause of death, knife, gun, or blunt instrument. If God's good to us, we'll find some special factor in the teeth, or a silver plate in a knee-cap, something unique to prove 'x' equals 'y'. But that doesn't help us know who's done it, who used the gun or the knife or the blunt instrument ... We'll check the statements again, looking for discrepancies. With luck we'll find two statements that just don't tally. Do you want to finish this last corned beef sandwich?"

The Sergeant shook his head. "I wouldn't mind another cup of tea if there's one going?"

"Help yourself."

Sergeant Bruton helped himself to tea, came back and sat down on the sofa. "Time you were going home," Aveyard said.

"I'm in no hurry. I'll hang on ..."

"... for what. For the miracle we need, but won't get! For Divine Revelation. Two weeks ago, somebody did something to

35

somebody, hit 'em, stabbed 'em, shot 'em ..."

"Not necessarily two weeks ago," Sergeant Bruton said. "Perhaps even during the last two weeks. Sometime between Olive Abbott making and the Bragg children fixing that Guy, and tonight."

"All right. Whenever it was—they strung him up on top of the Bonfire and left him for Harry Greaves' paraffin to finish off ..."

"It would have to be done during the night ..."

"All right, Jim, if you're so keen to work, write that down number one. Perhaps during the night, sometime during the past two weeks.

"Fact number two; It was done by somebody with access to Ulton village. Remember, that village isn't on a main road, and therefore anybody in the village would most likely have business in the village. It wasn't a casual passer-by !"

"Somebody from the village, you think?"

"What I *think* isn't important if this paragraph is headed *facts*," Jim Bruton said, reprovingly. "Olive Abbott is an old woman, but not so old she could sew a corpse into a suit of clothes without knowing what it was; and somehow I can't see an eighty-seven years old woman killing somebody who weighed as much as a bag of barley ... Latham says he tied the Guy to the stake with a chain, but can we believe him? Can we believe anything he says? What we must determine is, could the corpse have been in the Guy two weeks ago, or has the Guy been taken down at some stage and remade with a corpse inside?"

"Call your page 'suppositions', and I'll give you a third. If we discount the corpse having been there from the start, and think of the Guy being remade. The two lads had to have help to lift it, that's a fact, therefore we can assume it was too heavy for them. Therefore, we can assume Benny Latham was approximately correct when he said it weighed as much as a bag of barley. Whoever took the Guy down, re-stuffed it, and put it back up there, must therefore have been a man ..."

"We've had that before, Bill—a man, or a strong woman ... it's a dangerous supposition to make ..."

"Hell hath no fury, eh? Now I'll give you a question. All

36

right, let's assume somebody murders somebody, and has the inevitable problem of disposing of the body. He knows about the Guy, thinks to himself, that would be the perfect place. That bonfire'll get pretty damned hot, and nobody's going looking in bonfire ash to find a calcined skeleton. So he, or she, takes down the Guy, puts the victim in its place, and then what ...?"

"What does he do with the old Guy?"

"That's the question ..."

Both were silent for a moment. Then the Sergeant made a note on his pad. "I have another question for you," he said. "Everybody in the village knows about that Guy. It was dressed by Olive Abbott and put on public display. Olive Abbott walks past that Bonfire occasionally, and she doesn't need glasses, even at her age! What's she going to think if suddenly the Guy she dressed in a ...:" he flicked open his pad again and searched among his notes, "... in an old tweed suit, balaclava helmet, and gum boots ... suddenly turns up wearing different clothes. Whoever did the switch must also have changed the clothes ..."

"But the clothes were stitched together. So well stitched together that Latham couldn't swear if there was straw inside. Only that he 'got a feel of straw'. So whoever substituted the body for the Guy must have spent a long time doing it, considering he had to pull all that stitching apart to get the clothes to put on whoever he'd killed ..."

"With a knife, or a gun, or a blunt instrument ..."

"Or poison, or strangled with his bare hands or a rope, or even damned well frightened to death."

Jim Bruton sat still for a moment, glancing at his notes.

"One other possibility, too, Bill. We're assuming the corpse was placed on the pyre because the person who placed it there had killed it. But what if, let's just suppose for the moment, the dead person had died of perfectly natural causes, or even an accidental death, and the person or persons unknown who put it on the pyre were merely helping to dispose of it ... Just because we find a body, that doesn't mean to say we look for a murderer. We could be dealing with a suicide; imagine it, somebody commits suicide, yes, and let's take it a step further. Let's say person A had a life insurance policy, with a clause that makes the policy void in the case of a suicide. Now, person A commits suicide. His dependents find him. 'Oh dear,' they say, Dad's committed suicide! Bang goes the policy!' But if Dad had just disappeared, they could wait a few years, get a presumption of death, and the policy would pay off. So what do they do about Dad's body. If they bury it ..."

Both of them were thinking that bodies laid to rest in the ground can come to the surface again.*

"Or," he continued, "they could chuck it in the gravel pits, or else, they could stick it on top of the Bonfire ..."

"Where by tradition we dispose of our rubbish ...?"

"They burned Joan of Arc for some pretty odd reasons," the Sergeant said.

"Used to burn witches, of course ..."

"So we look for a heretic?"

"Or somebody who hates 'em ..."

Crime murders sleep; and through those waking thoughts before them twined a myriad madnesses, a tangled skein of speculations. Superintendent Bill Aveyard had a free-wheeling mind that could race beyond the snail's pace of a regulated investigation. Sergeant Jim Bruton needed facts, an opened pad, a sharpened pencil to record the minutiae of hearing, sight and smell, name, address, and date of birth suitably appended with opened and closed brackets, commas, and full stops. Burton could check a lie, Aveyard could smell a liar; they were complementary.

The telephone rang.

"Samson here. Not in bed, were you? They told me you'd gone home. Some people have all the luck."

"What have you found, Doctor?" Aveyard asked, ignoring the waspishness.

"Male, your victim was a mature male. Here's something that might help you; we found the residue of crystals in his joints ..."

"What should that tell me?"

"He had rheumatism ..."

"Badly ...?"

"Shocking. Flesh is a good insulator, you know. It takes
* See *Deadly Nightshade.*

38

many hours of incineration to destroy the cartilage between bones. That's where the crystals form, you know, in these cases ..."

"I didn't know," Aveyard said, feeling queasy. "Any positive identification marks?"

"I knew you'd ask me that. None that we can find. He hadn't been to a dentist for a long time, if ever. No signs of operations, no hernia marks, appendix, anything like that. He was fat. Gross would perhaps be a better word. He should have weighed two thirds of what he did. Height, five feet nine, no more. Broad shoulders, long arms. Spine curved, as if he'd done a lot of bending over at work. Very round shouldered. Office worker to judge from his musculature; he's never worked hard in his life!"

"No rings on his fingers? An inscribed watch in his pocket?"

"Nothing like that, worse luck!"

"So there's no help you can give us, not yet ...?"

"Your Sergeant will love this. Remember what I told you about rheumatism? Doctors keep records, you know. Put 'em through a computer and you'll find the twenty thousand or so mature males in the county who suffer from it!" Dr Samson said, as he hung up, still chuckling.

## SATURDAY MORNING

The village of Ulton awoke slowly, with a sense of outrage. Since no-one from the village was missing save Bert Dunkley, and he went *after* the discovery of the body, it stood to reason that whoever was put on the Bonfire had been brought from outside. A stranger, on the Ulton Bonfire! It would be difficult to say who started the rumour about Brian Sharp; perhaps Harry Greaves first had the idea on his way round with the letters; maybe it was Jenny Latham who earned pocket money delivering newspapers dumped off the first bus at the end of Ulton Lane; it could have been Richard Hopton, never called Dick, who still ladled milk from his father's herd to the folks of the old village. The rumour started innocently enough.

Brian Sharp, he's been away in London. What's he gone for? He went Friday, on the Birton bus, to take the train. People rode on the bus with him. Which people? Well, now you come to mention it ... He *was* seen walking to the bus, along Ulton Lane. Who saw him walking along Ulton Lane? That's easy. Stan Coulson, been to Birton, coming home in his car, passed Brian Sharp, stopped and had a word, when was he going to start concreting the pig yard? Brian Sharp was vague. "I'm just off to London, Stan. See if I can fit it in when I get back." "When's that likely to be?" Stan asked, but Brian was vague. "I reckon it'll be the Monday after next, if I get back in time." Brian Sharp had told Harry Greaves he was off to London, when he stopped his letters. He told Richard Hopton when he stopped his milk, half a pint a day and hardly worth walking up the path for. He told Bert Larrapin in the pub, when he gave him the spare key to look after. "Keep an eye on the place for me?" The cottage was old, two rooms downstairs, two rooms upstairs, thick thatch. Brian Sharp was thirty-five, a bachelor. Sheds at the back built to house the cows when the cottage was young now held bricks, cement, timber torn from old houses pulled down in their prime by young wives aching for easy washable plastic surfaces. If one of the village kids breaks a window, fetch Brian Sharp. Not that there are many kids to break windows. If your lavatory blocks and you can't get a wire round the 'S' bend, or the damp comes in or a window ledge has rotted under its thirty layers of paint, fetch Brian Sharp. He was short, wore a flat cap that had rounded its top like a bowler, always made of grey felted serge cloth. Little round man; off to London. What the devil would he do there?

The news was all round Ulton by smoky bacon breakfast time, which in the old part of the village is seven o'clock. Lie-abed Eastfield buys its bacon in plastic packs, unsmoked, from the Birton supermarkets; they'll get the news later. "Have you heard, Brian Sharp's missing! They say it was 'im on the Bon-fire. Who'd want to do a thing like that? You know he used to have girls in his cottage. Orgies, that's what he used to have there. No wonder somebody killed him. But why stick 'im on the fire? Best place for him, the rapist. They say it was the father of one of the girls. No wonder he never got married,

40

when he was having it all the time with anybody he could get in there ..."

Amy Dunkley riddled the grate in the Raeburn stove. The fire hadn't been banked with coal slack for the night the way she usually did, and the water in the cylinder started to boil. She drew a sink half full to cool down the storage tank, thought for one wild moment about having a bath. Having a bath, on a Saturday morning! She must be losing her mind. She'd had her bath Friday night, before the Bonfire, Friday night like she always did. Fred had gone up to bed about four o'clock. There was nothing else they could do. They'd been to see Olive; that was the place most likely for Bert to be. He couldn't go far, in November, without his trousers. She'd checked of course, and his jeans and the other pair he kept for best were in his bedroom closet. So was the suit Olive had bought him despite Amy's protests. She'd always been careful to treat Bert right, knowing in her heart his father was the man who'd held her down in the bottom of the hedge those years ago; Olive always took his side, accused them of being too strict. "He's only a lad," she'd say. Amy knew there was a kink in the boy; he'd stolen money from her purse several times and she'd said nothing to Fred. Was that her mistake? She cried whenever she thought about the cat Fred had brought home for her. Marmalade. It had loved to jump on her lap and be cuddled, a great comfort to her when Bert was particularly trying. Bert had taken a string and tied it round Marmalade's neck, then he flipped the string over the back of a chair he was sitting on, and dragged the cat as high as he could get it, up the back of the chair, until the cat's feet just couldn't reach the ground. She came into the room too late to save Marmalade. She hadn't dared tell Fred, for fear of what he'd do to the boy. She wept at the memory of poor Marmalade. She heard Fred stirring in the bedroom above her, took the kettle from the top of the Raeburn stove, and poured the boiling water into the tea-pot warm from the hot plate.

Fred came down in his trousers and shirt. "Bloody cold this morning," he said, only half awake.

41

"You should have stayed in bed, love," she said as she handed him a mug of tea. He stood with his back to the Raeburn, sipping it. "Gets right in your bones, the cold does," he said, gulping down the steaming tea. When he had emptied the mug she filled it again. He went to the cupboard, took out his bottle of whisky, and poured a tot into the tea. "That'll warm the old bones," he said. She looked at him. "You feel the cold more when you're worried," she said.

She had opened the stove doors wide and the room filled with warmth. He dragged a chair beside the stove, sat beside her, staring into the flames.

"I looked in his bed when I got up."

"I heard you in there."

"Where the devil can he be ...?"

"Cold and hungry," she said, tears in her eyes. He grabbed her hand. "Don't worry," he said, "he's in a barn somewhere, hiding in the hay. Warm enough. Bet he's asleep; he likes his kip. When he wakes up, he'll come round the back door, wanting breakfast ..."

"I've got some sausages," she said, "but there's only enough for one. I was saving 'em for you ..."

"Put 'em on one side for him," Fred said.


Francis Elks was on his knees on a hassock in the Church. He hadn't been to bed. "Dear God," he said, "Thou who sees all ..." Had he done right, reporting the boy? He could have waited until the excitement of the Bonfire had died down, taken the boy quietly to one side, and talked to him. But no! Foolishly he'd rushed to the boy's father, and the might of the Law had been invoked. The police have a frightening image to a young boy. Young boys don't understand that police, like parsons, are there to help. Young boys think the police an instrument of man's punishment, the parson an instrument of God's wrath. "Dear God," he asked, "help me see the way!" His knees were mortified after hours of kneeling on the hassock.

Morning light suffused the interior of the Church as if the walls and the ceiling glowed from within. Though there was no dramatic ray of light gleaming through the stained-glass windows, the altar he had erected at the feet of the chancel steps seemed imbued with a phosphorescence that compelled his attention. Was it a vanity to hope to reassemble the scattered remnants of a Faith by moving forward a focus of worship? What had he ever done for Bert Dunkley to give him faith? What good would moving the altar do to *him*? Francis Elks had known the boy all his life; he'd seen the wayward path the boy was taking. But what had he ever done to *help* the boy?

In his pride, Francis had hoped to unite the worshippers by bringing them towards himself and each other. This had been his mission. Worship had always been a separated act with a formalised and ritualistic communion; Esther Larrapin sat behind a pillar, Harry Greaves beside the font, Tom Bollard beneath the lectern. By what right had he, Francis Elks, taken away their sacred solitude in the House of God? His mission should have been outside the Church, not inside. Had he become too pre-occupied with the fabric of worship? One small boy was hiding somewhere in the village testing the acid of a small boy's fears. If one boy fled how many more must there be with a real need of understanding?

When had he last gone voluntarily into Eastfields; when had he taken his Mission there? Not one of the new villagers came to Church, but why had he abandoned them as materialistic pleasure-seekers?

He rose to his feet and walked briskly from the Church, not looking back at the altar radiant with light. Only when he approached the Rectory and smelled his breakfast bacon cooking, did he realise how completely he'd forgotten the dead man on the Bonfire. 'I meant to say a prayer for him,' he thought as he waved at Jo, looking out for him through the kitchen window.

Saturday morning in the village of Ulton. Seven o'clock and it's late for some. Stan Coulson hates cold mornings, but winter ploughing needs to be done, and he's opened up two furrows in the long field south of Home Farm. They're short of rain, the field's dusty where the plough bites and furrows crumble. Chemical fertiliser's good, cheap and convenient, but it flakes the soil something cruel. Stan could remember a day he'd pick up a handful of Long Meadow Field, as it was called, and the soil'd

43

ball in his hand fit to play cricket. Now it crumbled through his fingers; the nitrogen was there, certainly, just look at the crops, but where was the humus, where was the rich dark brown loam that fattened wheat, put cream in cows' udders, and made the plough blades hiss. Ploughing's a quiet dusty job now and since the worms are gone that used to aerate the soil, there are few birds about to follow the plough and keep you company. Once you couldn't drive a tractor without the constant caw of sea-gulls and God knows where they came from, so far inland. 'I think I'll retire next year,' Stan Coulson thought, as he switched off the tractor to walk back to Home Farm for his breakfast.

Saturday morning in the village and Harry Greaves opens the shop early in case anybody's desperate for a smoke; ten cigs and a box of matches. They'd never dream of buying a twenty packet, except on a Saturday afternoon late. They buy one stamp, to send the pools away each week. Harry chuckled as he remembered that the previous week Bill Hopton, sitting on two hundred acres of best grass keep, worth at a guess two hundred and fifty pounds an acre in good heart, had stood in the shop and brass-faced asked if he'd split a packet of laces. "One lace, Harry, that's all I need," he'd insisted.

"Go on! Make a pig of yourself! Buy a *pair*!"

In the end, he'd torn open the packet of two laces and sold Bill Hopton one. You can't change village folk; you'd be a fool to try. He switched on the alarm that sounded automatically whenever the door was opened, an innovation he'd installed when the brass bell on its spring finally gave up the ghost six weeks before, and went into the back room. Mug of tea, weak the way he liked it, with half a spoonful of sugar, and little milk; he sat at the kitchen table that served as an office and wearily pushed the multitude of post office forms into a pile at one side. He hated office work; sometimes wondered if it was worth while running a sub branch, with so much paper work to do. He drew forward the pad on which he'd written the items for the Youth Club barn-dance they were running that night, him and the Rector Francis Elks. Looking round his living room you would not have thought Harry Greaves a methodical man; but you'd have changed your mind if you'd seen his

44

list for the barn-dance, everything checked and double checked. The barn-dance was always held the night after the Bonfire, and always called a barn-dance. There had been a suggestion they rename it a Barbecue and Dance, but the parish council who financed it vetoed the more modern name. "Ulton's had a barn-dance ever since I can remember," Tom Bollard had said, "and I mean to use my vote to see it remains a barn-dance until the worms get me!" Refreshments were always provided with the entrance ticket; Mrs Elks' parkin, sausages, and bottles of lemonade.

"I can get a nice cheap line in hamburgers from the wholesaler." Harry Greaves, the newest council member, proposed. There was a shocked silence. "Or even frankfurters, in a roll ..." Harry knew when he was beaten. "Right, two gross of pork chipolatas it is ..."

It was all there, in his check list. Stan Coulson, a turkey for the raffle, and East Lodge Farm three chickens. Olive Abbott, a box of hand-made doilies, four cream cakes promised, six pots of assorted jams from Nancy Bollard, who made the best jam this side of Birton, and six pots of chutney from Amanda Blatsoe, the gamekeeper's wife.

The shop door buzzer rasped in his ear; the brass bell had made a homelier sound. Superintendent Aveyard was in the shop. "You're up and about early. You work long hours," Harry Greaves said by way of greeting.

"Almost as long as a postman!"

Harry Greaves waved him through into the back parlour. "I assume you've not come to buy anything? Pity, we do a nice range in sherbet lollies, six different flavours ...?"

Aveyard laughed. "I'm trying to cut down on my sherbet lollies!" he said.

When Aveyard was seated in the armchair by the stove, a cup of weak tea standing deliberately neglected beside him, Harry Greaves moved the pad from the centre of the table and sat down. "What do you want to ask me about?" he said, "the dead man on the Bonfire, Bert Dunkley who's gone missing, Bert Latham, you name it ..."

Aveyard thought for a moment. "When I'm on one of these jobs," he said, "I always seem to do well in the local shop. Tell me about the village of Ulton. Is this the sort of place you dump people on a Bonfire if their face doesn't fit?"

"I don't think the Bonfire had anything to do with us," Harry said, "but I could be mistaken. Bert Dunkley, well, that's different. A kid of eleven, gone as wrong as a kid can go. I wouldn't let him alone in this shop for a second or he'd have summat off the counter. He was a nasty, mean, vicious, horrible brat. And for why? He had two of the nicest parents you could wish for. Amy Dunkley, well she's a jewel, that woman. She'd do anything for that boy ..."

"Spoiled him perhaps? You hear a lot about mothers who are too good to their kids."

"No, there was none of that! She was strict with him when she should have been, but always in a kindly way. No, I wouldn't say she spoiled him."

"What about his Dad?"

"There again, a good solid man. A bit quick tempered, perhaps, but he tried hard to control himself. He's as strong as a bull, you know. I wouldn't like the back of his hand across my chops."

"Did he beat the kid?"

"A couple of times. But you've got to look further than that!"

"In which direction?"

"Olive Abbott for one. Now *she* spoiled the boy. He was what's the phrase, the apple of her eye! You can bet your last half-penny, if he was anywhere near this shop when she came to draw her pension, she'd buy him whatever he'd a mind to ask for. Sweets, toys, writing books, packets of stamps for his so-called collection. I've known her spend as much as five shillings out of her pension, and that's a lot of money."

"Does she have money, savings?"

"I'm not supposed to talk about that, you know. The contents of a savings book are supposed to be secret between the depositor and the government which I, as sub-postmaster, represent."

"All right, you've made your point. Now tell me, does she have savings?"

Harry Greaves smiled. "Right weevil you are, Superintendent.

I see we'll get on together! She's worked all her life, sewing. She used to make suits, coats for the local lads before they started going off to the town, and a lot of muck they buy there, I can tell you. She made every wedding dress that was ever used in this village for fifty years. Yes, and the bridesmaids' dresses too. She spends a lot, but she's made quite a bit. A lot of people'll be surprised when she dies. A *lot* of people. I'm witness to her Will; but don't ask me to talk about it, that'd be going too far ..."

"You said she spends a lot?" Forget the irrelevancies; for Olive Abbott to spend a lot stuck out like a sore thumb.

"Well, for an old lady her age and weight, for example, she eats a lot. And she smokes a lot. I've known her get through eighty cigarettes a week ..."

"On a pension ... And got enough put by to make a Will, *and* spend as much as five bob on sweets for a favourite kid ...?"

The investigation of a suspected murder is a feat of complex and detailed organisation. Nominally Detective Superintendent Aveyard was in charge, though he was answerable to the Detective Chief Superintendent and through him the Chief Constable of Birton. In other forces throughout the country, the Chief himself would have been directly concerned in the investigation, but the Chief Constable of Birton had his own ideas about giving early responsibility to his officers. The appointment of Aveyard to Inspector at an early age was typical, and though his promotion to Superintendent came as a surprise, everyone who knew him felt the elevation was justified.

An 'Incident Post' had been set up in the village schoolroom, supervised by Inspector Coates of B Division. Telephone lines were hurriedly installed during the night by a special section of the Post Office more used to county agricultural shows than the scene of a murder. At eight o'clock a van brought four typewriters, with girl staff to operate them on loan from A and C Divisions, and a Xerox copying machine. Inspector Coates knew from experience that before the case

47

was finished, the documentation could run to as many as a thousand pages.

Saturday morning in the village and strange cars drive silently along Ulton Lane and Church Street, to park in the school playground, round the back, out of sight. A furniture van, plain green, discharges a safe, a filing cabinet, and two filing clerks who've hitched a lift. Last to come out, but first to be plugged in for use, is an automatic vending machine that makes tea and coffee at five new pence a cup. "Where's Joe?" everyone asks. Joe has a key, inserts it in the front panel of the vending machine, and opens the door. Water all right. Heating element all right, plenty of paper cups, powdered sugar substitute, instant tea and coffee; it tastes like old leather washings but there's nothing like it when you're half way through reading a dry-as-dust scene-of-the-incident report. Joe connects the coin input to the coin output, winks at a girl standing nearby, shuts and locks the door. " 'Ave a go, luv," he says. She puts her coin into the machine, presses the button for coffee with extra milk and sugar, the paper cup drops down. There's a short pause, then the liquid begins. When the cup's full to brimming, she lifts the plastic window, takes the cup clumsily from between the stainless steel fingers that hold it upright, and starts to walk away.

"Here!" Joe says, surprised, "It's obvious you've never been on an incident!"

She looks at him puzzled. He presses the coin return and out pops her fivepenny piece. "One of the perks," he explains.

In the main room Inspector Coates sits behind the teacher's desk. A line of plain clothes men stands in front of him, handing in forms. As he receives them, the Inspector checks the name, and makes a tick against the side of the electoral roll. All the forms are the same, a list of the questions to which Superintendent Aveyard wants answers. A routine form of interrogation about as far from Sherlock Holmes and Sexton Blake as you can get, at least it ensures no vital question is missed. Provided, of course, the Superintendent has thought of everything. A large space on the back of the form is headed 'anything else the interviewer or interviewee might consider relevant to the incident?' In that space, a detective can write words that mean

48

promotion if he's extra alert.

When the Inspector has received the forms, he passes them across to Sergeant Stopes, sitting at the desk thirty years too small. On another desk beside him, a chart contains the numbered names of every person who lives in the village. Sergeant Stopes is interested in only one paragraph at the bottom of page two. 'Give the full names of anyone you saw and recognised at the scene of the Bonfire. Give descriptions of anyone you saw but did not recognise.' As each person is identified by other people, the numbers are cross-referenced. It takes three identifications to make the Sergeant lose interest in any one person. So far, a number of people have seen but not recognised a man wearing a duffle coat, who stood anywhere between five and six feet high, weighed between ten and fifteen stone, wore shoes, rubber boots, riding boots, and carried a rod, a walking stick, a riding crop and/or a single-barrelled shotgun.

Sergeant Stopes hurried across the schoolroom to the desk of Inspector Coates. "One odd bod turned up," he said, "the usual tall short dark fair light heavyweight, but they all agree he's a stranger, an adult male ..."

The Inspector smiled. "I wondered when you'd pick *him* up," he said. "Stranger in these parts. An American, staying with the Westerns. He was the one first shouted out the Guy was human. We saved him for the Superintendent!"


Saturday morning and the Westerns woke slowly, dragging themselves reluctantly from a short sleep after a night of late talking. Tongues loosen in the country without the seeping noise of a city's traffic to compete against; perhaps it's the lack of monoxide in the air; clean breathing stimulates the mind as much as the appetite. John Western's contemporaries crouched in Burnham boats, climbed unpronounceable mountains in Wales, rallied around the home counties in search of check points. John came to Ulton, tended a small garden, propped up the bar of the Pub, and swore that one day he'd install an inside toilet.

The first noise Julian Muller heard when he awoke was the coarse crooning of a pigeon on his window ledge. He lay

49

awake, listening, uncertain of where he was. Had he dreamed that the previous evening they'd found a body in a fire? Had he imagined it? His hands felt the rough texture of the unbleached cotton sheets Jeanne kept on the beds. He turned his head and caught the reflection of a line of sunshine on the curved body of the ewer and basin beside his bed. In the antique shops that line Third Avenue New York, you couldn't buy such a matching pair for fifty dollars. The bed in which he had slept was made of brass. He lay back in the unwonted luxury of this room, old when the *Mayflower* sailed. Bottle glass windows endowed the harsh winter sunlight with a soft greeny glow, the pattern on the wall crazed by the window pane's air bubbles. The air of the unheated bedroom was cold, and he was grateful for the warmth of the blankets and the woollen counterpane. He had awoken with the memory of the corpse, but despite himself he chuckled, lying in the bed. Minton ewers, bottle glass windows, woollen counterpanes, even their crimes have a Gothic air about them! he thought.

Jeanne had prepared breakfast for him when he went downstairs; thick porridge, bacon and eggs, toast, and Dundee marmalade, with a large pot of coffee.

"Where's John this morning?" he asked, as he sat down to his breakfast.

"Where he is every Saturday morning. Talking to his cactus plants. We shan't see him until the Pub opens!"


Bill Aveyard, standing on the pavement outside Harry Greaves' shop, is undecided where to go next. Left down Tingdene Way will bring him to the Church and the site of the Bonfire. A sweet but acrid smell still seems to hang over that area, but that could be all in the mind, couldn't it? The police have doused the fire, sifted the ashes, and now there's a heap of charcoal lumps and burned ends of sticks. They found nothing, of course. Benny Latham's lying since there's no sign of a chain among the ashes. Neither is there any wire that might have been used to lash the Guy to the stake. There are several bits of barbed wire, a coil of flex with the insulation burned off. The only conclusion they can reach so far is that Benny

50

Latham's lying. He must have tied the Guy with string, must have! But why tell a lie about a thing like that? Aveyard looked across the village green. Whoever constructed the heart of this village had an eye for landscape. The Big House, straight ahead, overlooking the village, but separated from it by well grown mature trees and a high stone wall. It's there, and you'd always know it. The trees are evergreen, luxurious conifers' with exotic foliage. Warm trees for a November morning. The Church on the left and in front of him framed the other side of the picture postcard view. Many differing textures, soft grass at his feet, small trees, thin whippy branches that move constantly like the arms of a conductor coaxing Delius from a still orchestra, stone walls on houses, cut in blocks and laid together with random lines that keep your eye within the structure, instead of zipping it off the way a continuous brick and cement line does. Thatch that spreads over the roofs of houses almost like a crinoline; doors and windows peeping out painted red and yellow but many without paint since they were fashioned from woods that don't need it. Chestnut window ledges, oak sills, beech door panels, purpose made by a craftsman's hands to stay young when his kid's kids grow old.

Saturday morning in Ulton, smoke curled out of chimneys, Bill Aveyard stood shivering on the edge of the village Green because it was cold and he was cold and death had pressed down its cold hands. Cold memory fades eventually. Next year they'd be saying—'that was where we found it, the Corpse in the Bonfire' or some such newspaper invented name. Young folk walking home at nights would draw their coats about them and scurry past the 'scene of the crime'. Misty legends are born and perpetuated, tradition starts cold where a life had ended. 'You'll see how the grass never grows there. That's where we laid 'im to rest.' Or, 'see how the grass grows, there, at his last resting place!' Death was acceptable only if it could be equated with peace, the end of suffering, a burden laid down at last. Death for Aveyard meant crime, the cold passionless retribution. The corpse belonged to the pathologist and the mourners, not to Aveyard. His concern was for the criminal who lived on when others had died.

He set off to walk briskly across the Green to the entrance

51

gate of Ulton Manor, home, so the electoral roll told him, of Arthur Newsome.

Roger Blatsoe had been up since five; a gamekeeper likes to know where his pheasants are sleeping, and Arthur Newsome, young Mr Newsome, would be out on Monday swearing blue bloody murder if Blatsoe couldn't put 'em up for him where he liked 'em to be, high, up and over. He was walking along Ulton Lane, southwards past Home Farm, towards his cottage on the left of the lane. He carried a shotgun crooked in one elbow, and two yellow labradors, Whisky and Brandy, trotted at his heels, their muzzles within inches of his knee ready to obey the silent command should his hand drop. A working dog's a dog, not a baby, and needs a master, not a loving mother. Roger Blatsoe uttered none of these juvenile phrases with which townsfolk smother lap-dogs, but as they walked along together, all three were in constant communication. The hand dropped. Brandy stopped and sat; Whisky saw the move and he too obeyed. Roger Blatsoe stopped.

"Good morning," Sergeant Bruton said.

"Morning."

"I was coming down to see you ..."

"Was you then?" Hand lifted. Whisky and Brandy stood, tails wagging. Gun dogs don't like too much sitting on pavements. They walked down the lane, all four of them. Sergeant Bruton didn't speak, waiting for Roger Blatsoe to make the overtures, if he wanted to. Many a man doesn't care to talk on the street; Bruton was in no hurry. They turned into the yard outside Blatsoe's house; Blatsoe opened the gate to let the dogs into their compound, checked they had a bowl of water. He opened the side door of the house, and went in. "In there," he said, pointing to a door to the right. He took off his green canvas twill shooting jacket, hung it on a peg in the small hall-way. Hat on a peg above it. He pulled off the rubber boots he'd been wearing over his coarse woollen stockings and breeches, then slipped his feet into a pair of brown leather boots from a rack of boots standing on the floor beneath the coat-rack. "I'm in, Mother," he called. His wife answered from the kitchen. "I've brought a policeman with me; shall us give him a cup of tea or summat?"

He went into the parlour where Sergeant Bruton was standing in front of the empty fireplace. The room was cold but Blatsoe didn't seem to notice it. Sergeant Bruton was glad of his coat. He looked around the room. Small clues are often vital. General atmosphere, suffocatingly neat. 'A place for everything and everything in its place.' No dust of course. Very few ornaments. No flowers. No knick-knacks, ash-trays, pot dogs, the like. He doesn't smoke, his wife doesn't smoke and his two kids, Sophie and Betty, don't use this room. No homework, no books, papers, pencils, drawing instruments. Sofa and two chairs covered in cretonne; a table's dully polished wood matched the beams. Inglenook fireplace rarely lighted these days. Fire irons on brass hooks, that have been polished with elbow grease every week for well over a hundred years. Carpet's seen better days; no pictures on the wall, not even *the Monarch of the Glens* or *When did you last see your Father?* Clock on the mantelpiece covered with a glass cylinder, without a speck of dust. The clock goes, but then, it would, wouldn't it, wound up ritually on a Sunday night.

Roger Blatsoe unlocked the door built into the wall. In a cupboard were a half-dozen shotguns, three Lee Enfield .303 rifles, a .22, and three pistols. He slotted the shotgun he had been carrying into the cupboard, which he closed and locked, using a key hanging on a leather thong from the belt around his breeches. Bruton knew Blatsoe'd clean the gun as soon as he'd left—he was obviously not the man to leave a damp barrel to rust.

"Right, what shall us talk about?" Blatsoe asked, as he eased himself into a chair. The Sergeant sat on the other chair, unable to relax. It'd take a bomb to shake Roger Blatsoe.

"What can you tell me about the Bonfire, about the body that was found on it, young Bert Dunkley, the village in general ...?"

"What's young Bert go to do wi' it?"

"Nothing so far as we know."

"Then why are you asking about him?"

"Frankly, I don't know. There's a confession for you, a

policeman who admits he doesn't know! But we can't afford to overlook any possibilities ..."

"You're groping in the dark?"

"You could say that!"

The tea arrived and they drank it. They talked together for twenty minutes or more, but there was nothing Roger Blatsoe could tell him about the Bonfire he didn't already know. There was little he could say about the village itself that wasn't already common knowledge; he had little to do with village folk. "That comes o' being a gamekeeper," he said. "It's like I imagine being a policeman to be. You can't make friends because you never know who the next poacher's going to turn out to be. Many a man never stole in his life, wouldn't dream of stealing. Church wardens, some of 'em, respectable people every way you look at 'em, but show 'em a cock pheasant in the bushes and they can't keep they hands to theyself. Why should that be, Sergeant, what's special about poaching pheasants ...?"

Sergeant Bruton had no answer. How many people steal pencils, rubbers, envelopes, paper clips from the office in which they work?

"Time was we spent half our lives in the hedges, waiting for the village lads to creep by with a bag and a snare. Nowadays people buy pheasants, aye, and can afford 'em on today's wages. But we still get the lad who can't keep his hands off. Mostly nowadays my job's hatching eggs, and carrying corn and water to where the hen-birds are standing. Spoonfed, that's what today's pheasants are. That's why the taste is going out of 'em, but don't let on I said so! It makes it even worse to know you've reared the little buggers, and somebody pinches 'em! Like they was all your own family!"

"But you don't object to them being shot out of the sky?"

"That's a natural death for a bird, isn't it? Like somebody dying of old age, or even being knocked down by a motor car, that's natural. But for example, being killed in a war, that's unnatural, and we resent it, and we'd do anything to stop it. Like I'd do anything to stop any bugger having my pheasants ..."

* * *

Saturday morning in the village and the long day stretched ahead for Arthur Newsome, who could never sleep after five o'clock. Drink didn't help; years ago he could sit in the library half the night with a bottle of port, and by three o'clock be ready for six hours of deep sleep. Alas, port was no longer effective, sleeping pills didn't work, and Arthur Newsome lay awake after five o'clock wondering what to do with the long day ahead. His early morning thoughts always followed the same direct path; 'Arthur Newsome, you've been an anachronism. You've owned two thousand acres of prime land in one of the most fertile shires of England, and you're said to be a gentleman, so by definition you belong to the landed gentry; but what happened to all the rest of it? Why didn't you sit on the bench as a magistrate, why didn't you marry and raise a family, why isn't your house gay and sparkling with dances and barbecues and servants with pink shining cheeks? Why not, Arthur Newsome, bachelor at fifty-two and growing grumpy, why not?'

Ulton Hall was a finely preserved House built in the hey-day of shire architecture as a hunting lodge for a family with a town house in Berkeley Square. It had twenty bedrooms and twice as many stables, a ball-room, a billiard room in which two hundred of Charles Stuart's men reputedly slept before the Battle of Naseby. You could seat five courting couples *and* a chaperone inside the massive inglenook of the dining-room fireplace where oxen had been spit roasted; the minstrels' gallery accommodated twelve men, harp and spinet, and the centre dining table was made from one plank of oak forty feet long, five feet wide, and three inches thick matured for sixty-seven years after the tree had been felled. No-one knew how long the tree had been growing, but tradition was you felled it when a boy was born, used part of it for his coffin when he died. Once these rooms echoed to the sound of boots; shooting boots in coarse brown leather, hunting boots in black kid with a brown suède leather top, dancing boots of 'patent' doe skin, war boots spurred for the battle with jingling accoutrements. Once elegant ladies wore wasp waists and breasts sprouted from confinement; wives lay in the big bedroom and served the Master a baby every year, a rip-snorting proud rapscallion of a boy, or a sloe-eyed haughty devil-may-care girl who snatched her youthful pleasures from the back of a horse or the page of a dance-card, before duty and the demand for progeny laid her flat on her back while a man's man in a man's world rose high, up and over.

Arthur Newsome was twenty-one when war broke out; he joined the Northamptonshire Regiment and went immediately to France. When the war ended he was a full Colonel stationed at the War Office in London and had never seen the enemy. During the war in London he met and instantly fell head over heels in love with the American wife of an officer of the US Marines. A beauty, she had wit, poise and charm beyond anything Arthur Newsome had encountered. At the end of the war, however, she returned quickly to wait for her husband in Minnesota, and Arthur retired to Northamptonshire to live on inherited income. His father, always a considerate man, gave the entire estate to Arthur to avoid death duties, then thoughtfully waited the requisite legal period of five years before drowning with his wife and five other passengers when the yacht in which he was touring the Caribbean sank with all hands, off Kingston, Jamaica.

Arthur had sufficient capital and income to keep him in considerable luxury but he had no heirs. The land was let to tenant farmers, with clauses in the leases which preserved the shooting rights, his only passion. The House was cared for, in the modern way, by a cleaning company from Birton, on an annual contract. The garden was looked after by a landscape gardening company, also from Birton. The only staff Arthur maintained as direct labour were Roger Blatsoe, gamekeeper, Dodson and Sylvia Bragg. Dodson was butler, major domo, and general supervisor, Sylvia was housekeeper, personal maid, cook and bar-tender.

Arthur Newsome rose at half past five, said his usual prayer, "Please God let me die quickly," plugged in the percolator Sylvia Bragg had left charged the previous evening and made a cup of coffee which he always drank black and without sugar. Then he took a long and leisurely bath drugged with sleep and distressed by the dreams of the night. After his bath he opened the letters of the previous day, and answered any that needed it. Often his only correspondence was with his accountant in Birton. His 'office work', as wryly he put it, was finished by nine o'clock when Sylvia Bragg served his breakfast. The menu never changed. Every Monday, Wednesday, and Friday of the open season he would dress in breeches, boots, a woollen shirt and a jacket, and go to meet Blatsoe for the day's shooting.

Saturday morning, and Bill Aveyard tolled the front door bell of Ulton Hall. Dodson Bragg opened the door, nodded when he saw the Superintendent and led the way into a high-vaulted room on the right. Each wall was covered by glass-fronted cupboards containing books. Three vast armchairs stood too far apart for conversation and into the surface of three tables beside them had long ago been carved in bas-relief the Ulton coat of arms. Bill Aveyard let his eye run along the books; all were dust free and most bound in leather. The floor was of wood-blocks laid in an elaborate pattern of marquetry and the leaded windows hung with heavy plum velvet curtains on ornamental brass ringed rails.

It was a room in which Cuban and Jamaican cigars had been smoked and old French Armagnac drunk, while men in velvet smoking jackets indulged the pleasures of the mind and a mild distaste for anything that hadn't first been said in Greek or Latin. It was a room suited to a thinker, a man with a passion for old truths and immutable logic.

Dodson Bragg, ill at ease, muttered, "Sit down, if you've a mind to." Five minutes passed before Arthur Newsome appeared in the doorway, dressed in a thorn-proof tweed suit, gazing at the Superintendent through long-sighted eyes hard to focus to the nearness of objects in this enclosed room.

"I don't usually grant interviews," he said courteously, "but Mr Bragg tells me you're a policeman. How very curious! I don't think I've actually talked to a policeman before!"

Detective Superintendent Bill Aveyard, youngest to hold the rank on the Birton Police Force, apprehender of villains of all types and styles, felt six inches tall.

"Have you come to talk about the pheasants?" Arthur Newsome said, seating himself in one of the chairs.

## CHAPTER NINE

Aveyard and Bruton met again in Aveyard's car, parked in Ulton Lane near the entrance to the new houses on the estate called Eastfields.

"Anything?" Bruton asked.

Aveyard shook his head. "Young Mr Arthur's been dead for twenty years if you ask me ..." They sat in the front seat of the car, Bruton with his pad open on his knee. He turned over the page he'd headed with Arthur Newsome's name. "Give me the details," he said. Aveyard looked down the street composing his thoughts. "He went to the Bonfire, as usual. Saw the usual people there, stayed ten minutes, and left. He didn't see the Guy collapse. He didn't notice anything out of the ordinary. He spoke to Dodson Bragg and Sylvia Bragg, to Sophie and Betty Blatsoe, his employees' kids. He said good evening to a lot of other people but couldn't tell me their names. He walked from the Hall, walked back."

"What time was this?"

"He doesn't remember. He never carries a watch."

"But he must have clocks in the Hall ...?"

"He has, but they're all priceless heirlooms and he won't have them interfered with. Dodson Bragg winds them every week but he's forbidden to 'tamper' with them. The clock specialist comes once a year, in December. I checked, and all the clocks show different times. How can a man live like that, Jim?" Aveyard asked, perplexed.

"It helps if your father leaves you a few million!"

Aveyard sighed. "Oh, what the hell! You get anything out of Blatsoe ...?"

"Nothing I could put my finger on, though I got a feeling he was holding back. He seemed a worried man!"

"Did he tell you about the pheasants?"

"About hand rearing 'em, all that stuff ...?"

"No, about somebody pinching 'em ..."

"Oh, he mentioned that, in passing ..."

"*Mentioned* it. Arthur Newsome told me he's losing a score or more a week!" Aveyard said.

"No wonder he was worried. I knew there was something."

"We can pass it on to Division; whoever's lifting 'em must have found a market for 'em."

"Just think," Bruton said, "how pleasant it'd be to have to cope with a simple case of pheasant stealing!"

"Something to get your teeth into ..."

Bruton put down his pad, half turned in the car to look at the Superintendent. Though Aveyard was only half his age, Jim Bruton had an enormous respect for his ability and integrity. Bruton knew his own limitations; he was a careful slow thinking man who prided himself in his attention to detail. He knew he'd never even make the rank of Inspector. Bill Aveyard was the young breed of policeman, university educated, broad minded to appreciate the human needs of the criminals they dealt with, but flexible to appreciate that modern crime can come in strange packages. In Bruton's early days on the police force, people stole from poverty, or hunger, murdered from jealousy, greed or anger. You didn't get the involved psychological killings you get today, he thought, or the 'violence without apparent cause' that seemed the worst modern disease. You got queer and fanciful ones all right, respectable men who went quietly insane and dropped numerous wives into beds of lime, or worse, jealous women who poisoned their husbands over the years with drops of a herb somebody mixed secretly for them, or rat poison from the chemists; but somehow, there seemed to be a lot more weird crime these days, some of it organised, much of it apparently pointless.

"I don't mind admitting I'm completely baffled!" Aveyard said. "Firstly, there's the difficulty of getting the body to the top of that Bonfire without being seen. Secondly, there's the inefficiency! Fancy tying the damned thing so it'd fall down as soon as the fire got started!"

"If it'd been properly secured, we'd never have known it was there ..."

"Thank God for small mercies. None of this makes sense to me, Jim! Let me read your notes. Perhaps that'll do something for me!"

He sat hunched in the driving wheel, flipping through the detailed notes Bruton had taken. Bruton sat still and quiet, watching him, ready with any supplementary information, though he'd have been surprised if Aveyard had needed to ask questions. He prided himself on his note writing.

"Usual petty crime," Aveyard said as he shut the notebook. "That man Latham's obviously giving us a story; missing person, lead pinching—that's for the local lads. But I can't see anything in there for us. And what's even worse, I can't see a new line of enquiry, can you?"

Bruton shook his head. "We're checking all the doctors, but I don't expect much to come of that. I'll go down to Birton and read the list of people reported missing ..."

Both sat without speaking. Neither liked the admission they'd just made, that for once they were bereft of ideas—how had Blatsoe put it, 'groping in the dark'.

An ambulance had turned into Ulton Lane, and came rushing towards them, its blue light flashing. Both watched it idly for a moment, registering the fact but drawing no conclusions. The ambulance turned right, down Mann Crescent, into the Eastfields estate. Aveyard turned the key to start his engine and drove down Mann Crescent. The ambulance was parked outside number 4 Mann Way. As their car approached, the back doors of the ambulance were opened, and two men jumped out with a rolled stretcher. They hurried into the house. Aveyard stopped his car in front of the ambulance, got out and walked back. Within minutes the two ambulance men came out of the house carrying a woman wrapped in blankets. Several people had appeared from adjacent houses and were standing in a knot by the gate.

"It's Mrs Robinson," one of them said loud enough for Aveyard to hear. Sergeant Bruton had come from the car. "Stand back," he said, "stand back there and let 'em get through!"

61

The watchers moved slowly as cattle, and the ambulance men came through the crowd and slid the stretcher into the back of the vehicle.

Aveyard was walking up the path and had nearly reached the door when it opened. Dr Samson stood talking to a man old enough to be the father of the woman who'd been carried out.

"You got here quickly," the Doctor said, "I only telephoned a couple of minutes ago and they said you were out of radio contact ..."

"My radio's on the blink. They're fixing it this morning. I saw the ambulance. What is it ...?"

"You'd better come in," Dr Samson said, eyeing the gawping crowd by the gate. Aveyard beckoned to Sergeant Bruton, who walked down the path and into the house.

"This is Mr Robinson," Dr Samson said, "and that was his wife."

"Was ...?"

"Sorry. I mean, is his wife. You'll have to forgive me if I'm a little woolly; I've been up all night with that corpse of yours!"

Stanley Robinson was fifty-six, but looked seventy. He was dressed in a pair of trousers too large about the waist, hanging from him on braces. He had pulled on a shirt, but failed to tuck it in and the tail flap was hanging. He hadn't brushed his hair or put in his upper set of teeth. Sergeant Bruton knew this wasn't the first time he'd seen Stanley Robinson, though as yet the name or the face didn't mean anything specific. Sergeant Bruton took him into the sitting room.

"You were saying ..." Aveyard prompted the Doctor. His face was grey, he looked exhausted.

"I sent for you. Well, I phoned in, and they told me you were out here somewhere working, and they'd contact you. That woman's been poisoned, and from the looks of her, she's had enough to kill several people!"

"Can you tell me what the poison was?"

"Arsenic, I think. We'll make certain of course!"

"How did she get it? Cornflakes, in a cup of something?"

"No, it had been injected, and very clumsily at that."

62

"Where?" Aveyard asked.

"In her back. She couldn't possibly have done it herself!"

"Any idea when? Even a rough idea ..."

"You do like to push me ... I'd guess about an hour and a half ago."

Aveyard walked to the sitting-room door. "Would you come back in here Mr Robinson?" he asked, "and you, Sergeant."

Robinson stood just inside the door so that Bruton had difficulty getting past him. He seemed about to speak but Aveyard stopped him. "Don't say anything, Mr Robinson, not a single word." He turned back to the Doctor. "Who was in the house when you arrived?"

"Mr Robinson. He said they'd been alone. It was he who called me. There's a reason for that, but I'd rather not go into it at the moment."

Aveyard thought for a moment before he spoke again. "Let me make certain I've got this absolutely right. You have reason to believe that approximately ninety minutes ago a poison suspected as being arsenic was administered to Mrs Robinson in such a manner she could not have done it herself, and at a time when she was reportedly alone in this house with her husband, Mr Robinson. You have discovered no trace of the syringe or whatever instrument was used for the injection. Is that correct?"

"Yes."

"Mrs Robinson was found in a coma, and was unable to speak to you?"

"She didn't say a word."

"Where was Mrs Robinson when you arrived?"

"Sitting in that chair." The doctor indicated the armchair which stood incongruously in the kitchen. "I took her into the sitting room to conduct my examination ..."

"In the presence of Mr Robinson?"

"Yes, he helped me with his wife. To carry her through, I mean. He stayed while I examined her."

"And he hasn't been out of your sight since?"

"Only just now, when he went with Sergeant Bruton into the sitting room again."

"Can you give me any idea of Mrs Robinson's condition?

Is she, er, likely to die?"

The doctor looked at Stanley Robinson. "I don't like predictions of that sort!"

"Let's have the truth, Doctor," Stanley Robinson said.

"I don't think she has any hope of survival ..."

Sergeant Bruton stood in front of Robinson. "Stanley Robinson," the Sergeant said, "is that your name?"

"Yes, and I know the form so get on with it!"

"We have reason to believe that an offence has been committed. We would like to ask you questions about this offence. You are not obliged to say anything unless you wish to do so but what you may say may be put into writing and given in evidence. Is that clearly understood?"

"You're not charging me?"

"Since you know the form you realise I'll use a different caution if ever we decide to charge you. For the present, you'll be assisting us with our enquiries."

"I didn't do it," Stanley Robinson said, his manner controlled, "and I don't know how it happened. If the doctor says it's arsenic, well you'll find arsenic in my greenhouse. It's still the best thing for getting rid of caterpillars, but I *didn't give it to my wife!*"

"Tell us what happened?" They work as a team. Bruton asks the questions, Aveyard watches, listens more to inflections than to the actual words used. Many a man gives himself away, not so much by what he says, but by the way he says it. How many men tell a lie with a rising inflection at the end of a sentence. How many men pause after they've told a lie, often re-tell it, thinking emphasis will make it doubly convincing.

"I don't know what happened."

Doctor Samson touched Aveyard's arm. "All right if I go," he whispered. Aveyard nodded. "I'll ring you if there's anything we need," he said.

"Not before one o'clock if you can avoid it. I'm going to try to get some sleep!"

"All right," Sergeant Bruton said, "suppose we sit down and take it slowly." He sat in a chair beside the table. Stanley Robinson sat on the arm of an armchair, but Aveyard remained standing, above his eyeline. "Now, when did you first know anything had happened?"

"I came downstairs for my cup of tea shortly after six. I made the tea. I took a cup to my wife as usual, then I went outside."

"What for?"

"I always take my tea into the greenhouse to drink it. I always do ..."

"You can't say *always*, can you? This house is only about eighteen months old ..."

"Yes, but everywhere I've lived, I've always had a greenhouse, and I've always taken my wife a cup of tea, then gone to drink my own in the greenhouse ..."

"I'm labouring this point," Sergeant Bruton said, "because I want you to understand how accurate you need to be. How careful in your choice of words ..."

'Good man,' Aveyard thought. It was a system they'd developed between 'em. If a man tries to volunteer a statement, never let him get through it in one go. Chances are that if he *volunteers* a statement, he may well have *learned* it. If you make him re-examine it, you're more likely to get something of value out of him. Look at Stanley Robinson. Already he's rattled, and that's good, because it means he's off guard. There are lots of ways of doing it. One is to make him lose his temper, another, the one the Sergeant was now using, is to nag him about the meaning of a word.

"How long have you been married Mr Robinson?"

"Eighteen months. We were married into this house."

"So you can't say, you've always taken your wife a cup of tea, can you?"

"Damn it, you know what I mean," Stanley Robinson shouted, exploding into anger. Good. Good. It all helps.

"Yes, we *know* what you mean," the Sergeant said, "but we want to make certain you *say* what you mean. For the past eighteen months, since you lived in this house, you've taken your wife a cup of tea in bed, and then you've gone into the greenhouse to drink your own cup of tea ... is that right?"

"Damn you, that's what I've been telling you!"

"All right, Mr Robinson. No need to lose our temper, is there? Carry on, what next?"

Stanley Robinson controlled himself with a visible effort. "I stay about half an hour with that first cup. When I come back into the house, my wife always ..."

The Sergeant interrupted him. "What's your wife's first name?"

"Helen. Well, Helen always ..."

"Helen, eh? And how old is she ...?"

"Twenty-four. Let me get on with what I'm saying, will you. I can't get it out if you interrupt all the time!"

The Sergeant was silent.

"Well, can I get on with what I was saying ...?"

"You want me to speak now? Yes, Mr Robinson, yes, get on with it!"

'Don't overdo it, Sergeant,' Aveyard thought; 'you've done a good job of breaking him down, but don't overdo it ...'

"Where was I?" Stanley Robinson asked, "you've made me lose my train of thoughts!"

"*When I come back into the house my wife always,*" the Sergeant said without hesitation.

"She's usually got my breakfast ready, and to save you asking, I have a bit o' bacon on toast, and I like it well done!"

"And she had your breakfast ready this morning?"

"I didn't come into the house. I mean, it wasn't like usual; I was sitting in the greenhouse when she came and banged the door open. She was ill. 'Get the doctor, bloody quick,' she says. I picked her up, and rushed back into the house with her, and laid her out on this sofa, and it seemed like she was half dead, and I kept asking her 'what's wrong' but she couldn't answer me, seems like she was scared out of her wits or something, and then she seemed to be in a coma so I rang Dr Samson."

"Why Doctor Samson?"

"Because he's my Doctor."

"But when you telephoned his number they must have told you he was out! They must have given you another number to ring him, in Police Headquarters!"

There was an outside line to the path. lab. that didn't go through the switchboard. The number was not listed, and only policemen and pathologists knew it to use in emergencies during a case.

"I spoke to his wife. The Doctor's wife. She gave me the number to ring."

"Why?" It would have to be something special. Doctors' wives protect their husbands. Any patient ringing when her husband was out would be given the number of whichever of his junior partners was on duty that morning.

"Because she knew me!"

Aveyard put his hand on Bruton's shoulder. 'Leave this one,' the pressure said.

"Where did you live before you came here?" the Sergeant asked, responding instantly to Aveyard's unspoken message. He too had seen the change in Stanley Robinson. Now he was sitting upright in his chair and ran his hand through his hair to straighten it. He seemed to be coming out of the state of shock in which they'd first found him. He got up and went to the sideboard. On it was a glass; he reached into the glass, fished out his top set of teeth and clamped them into his mouth, biting on them to make them fit properly. When he turned round to face them again he'd found a new confidence. He sat on the armchair again, still leaning forward, but now alert.

"Can you describe your wife's condition to me again?" the Sergeant asked. "How was she when you first saw her at the door of the greenhouse?"

Stanley Robinson smiled, but there was no humour in it. "You've got a good memory; use it! I've nothing to add to what I said before and I know this trick to get me to repeat something so you can trip me up. I refuse to say anything else until I've had a chance to talk to a lawyer, and if you know a good one in Birton it'll save me asking Dr Samson ..."

"You think you need a lawyer, do you?" Aveyard asked.

Stanley Robinson nodded.

"Why?"

"You'll find out, when you hear from the Leeds police about Stanley Robinson, formerly of Filey Way, Crossgates."

# CHAPTER TEN

Esther Larrapin had just finished sweeping out the pub when Aveyard went there, just after eleven o'clock.

"Seems a shame, doesn't it," she said to him, "we've been here twenty years, and now the brewery's kicking us out and putting a manager in. They want our share of the profits as well as their own. Herbert's built this pub from scratch. When we first came here, it was all oil lamps, and you'd be lucky if you had three in the bar of an evening. Herbert used to do a bit of painting in those days; very good at it he was. He came here, really, to give us somewhere to live while he got on with his painting. I never wanted a pub, but I was quite prepared to go anywhere Herbert wanted."

"You've never called him Bert?"

"Just you try it and you'll get a backhander! No, funny thing, he *made* this pub, put it on the map as you might say, and all because of an accident ..."

Herbert came through to the back room from the bar, a polishing cloth in his hand. "Give us another, will you love," he said, "this one's sopping wet through!"

She took a linen cloth from a pile in a cupboard. "I was just telling the Superintendent here about how you put the pub on the map," she said.

He laughed. "Oh, aye, that old story ..."

"I wouldn't mind hearing it," Aveyard said. Let people tell you their favourite anecdote and they'll go on and tell you other things too. Sometimes you had to be patient, wondering when they'd get to anything that really interested you, but usually it was worth while.

"When we first came this pub was dead scruffy. Three barrels behind the bar, mild, brown and bitter. No pumps or anything like that. One day a fella came in quick and asked for a pint and I tapped it without looking. I was keen to get back to my painting, you see. Well, to cut a long story short, the beer was cloudy and when he complained, I don't know why, but quick as a flash I said 'oh, that's the new blend the brewery's serving, called Strong and Cloudy!' Well, the fella drunk it, had another, and came back that week-end bringing all his pals, for a pint of 'Strong and Cloudy'. We got quite a name for it. When the brewery got to hear they had a fit; the head brewer himself came out and played hell. 'I've spent all my life making beer clear, and you go and sell it "strong and cloudy"' he said. Well the brewery didn't know what to do. I mean I had as many as a hundred customers here, Rugby Club on Saturday nights, packed out Sunday dinner times ... In the end the brewery remade the pub for us, put electric lights in and a new bar and redecorated the place and installed these pumps. Of course, I had to agree to 'discontinue' the Strong and Cloudy! But by then I'd got my steady stream of customers and I was making a good living ..."

"And the painting?" Aveyard asked.

"Oh, I gave that up. I was never really cut out for it, you know. It was more of a hobby with me, and I'd 'a been in the workhouse if ever I'd tried to make my living at it ..."

Herbert unfolded the dry linen cloth, and laughed again. "Funny the way it all happened, all because of an accident." He went out of the kitchen, back towards the bar. Esther watched him go; Aveyard could sense the great affection in her.

"The pub's been good for Herbert," she said. "He was unhappy trying to paint. He's never looked back since the days of Strong and Cloudy. Of course, we don't get many of the Birton trade any more, but we do quite comfortably off the locals. They all come in here, you know, and we get the catering for all the weddings, and parties, and the fête, and the barn-dance. It seems a shame the brewery's chucking us out to put in a manager as won't have the same interest!"

"If all the locals come in here, you must have a good idea what goes on in the village?"

"There's not much my Herbert misses!"

"Does he have any idea who the corpse on the Bonfire might have been ...?"

She thought a moment, then looked up at the Superintendent. "In a village, if you know what I mean, there's seldom anything straight out. It's all rumours and suspicions, it'll surprise you to learn some of the things that go on ..."

"Such as?"

"It's hard to put your finger on 'em, exactly. Take the business about the Bonfire. Well, in a curious way, that's typical, that is. Bizarre. Not straightforward. I mean, it's such a commonplace village, if you ask me. Everybody acts alike, talks alike, why, they even look alike. You've seen most of the girls, the ones in the old village from the old established families here, the Coulsons, Lathams, Bollards, Blatsoes, Abbotts—well not so much the Abbotts now Olive's on her own—but my husband and I have a name for 'em. We call 'em the Ulton Lumps. They're all the same physical type—I can never remember if its endomorphic or ectomorphic but there was an article about it in one of the Sundays."

"Fat women ...?"

"Well, not just fat. It's the type of shape like a balloon, people who can never be slim no matter how little they eat. The men are the same, short and dumpy, broad across the shoulders, barrel chested ..."

"Stanley Robinson's not that type, nor is Helen an Ulton Lump ..." Aveyard said, to get her back on the track.

"Ah no, but they're not Ulton folk, are they. Of course, I could have told you a long time back *they'd* never make a go of it. Winter and Spring, that's what they are. Look at him, sloppy, slovenly, he's a man who sometimes seems twice his age. Look at her, young and lively. She couldn't sit in that house of an evening if you paid her. Not her! She has to be out enjoying herself. While he'd be happy to spend his life in that greenhouse. What she ever saw in him to marry, I'll never know. And now look what's happened. He's gone and done for her!"

"That's all rumour, Mrs Larrapin. Nobody knows yet what has happened!"

"Believe me, I've seen something like this coming for a long time. They're against nature, these winter and spring romances. Take me and Herbert, same ages, same backgrounds, same

70

interests. But what could a lass of twenty-four have in common with a man of fifty-six, and 'im an old fifty-six at that!"

"Who did Mrs Robinson do her 'enjoying' with, if he was always in the greenhouse?" She may be willing to repeat rumours, but that doesn't mean to say she'll give you the gossip. A person needs a touch of malice for that, and there's little malice in Esther Larrapin.

"Common knowledge, that is," she said. "Aubrey Bollard had her out a time or two, but I reckon that was innocent. What you might call a smokescreen! I reckon she was going strong on the quiet with Brian Sharp. You haven't met him yet, I imagine, since he's away in London for the week-end."

"There was a rumour that Brian Sharp was, well you know, the corpse we found on the Bonfire ..."

"Don't you believe that old wives' tale!"

"Why not?"

"If for no other reason than that Brian Sharp knew how to look after himself too well. Like I said, things in a village are never straight. Brian Sharp just wasn't the sort to get himself put onto a Bonfire. Some angry husband'll do for Brian Sharp, one of these days, or some angry dad ..."

"You wouldn't like to mention a couple of names ...?"

She laughed at him, her voice tinkling merrily. She'd been sitting at the table, drinking her late morning coffee. She took his cup and hers and put them into the sink before replying.

"Well, if you don't bring me or my Herbert into it ...?"

"I promise you that ..."

"Daphne Bollard. Last year she had an abortion. In London. Iris Latham. Betty Frobisher from Eastfields; her husband's away a lot of the time. And then, of course, there's Helen Robinson. She was twenty-four."

"Brian Sharp likes 'em young ..."

"He likes 'em. Full stop!"

"You never had a daughter ...?"

"Thank God. Two sons, William and Walter, been enough for us. Our William'll be married next year to a nice girl from the other side of Birton. He's got a good job with the Anglia Insurance Company, and I for one am pleased to see him get out of the village. This is a closed community, Superintendent, and it needs fumigating. We all thought a bit of life'd come when they built up Eastfields, but it hasn't. Eastfields is, well what do they call it, a dormitory suburb. The people sleep there, nothing else. They have gardens the size of a pocket handkerchief, and houses you couldn't swing a cat in; they all work in Birton or Corby or Rushden, and they come home for meals and a sleep. The biscuit people send a bus every morning, and half the wives lock their front doors and go out to work; there's more colour televisions on HP in Eastfields than there are bless you's in charity. And motor cars they spend all Saturday cleaning. There's not one of 'em in the Women's Institute, or the Mothers' Guild, or turns out for the cricket team or comes to the barn-dance. Or uses this pub for that matter ... No, I'm glad my boy's getting out of it, and when next year comes and the brewery kicks us out of this pub after all these years, I shall go myself without regret."

"Amen to that," Bert Larrapin said. He'd come unnoticed from the bar and stood just inside the kitchen door. "What about a quick 'un before I open up?" he said, holding a glass of new drawn beer in his hand.

# CHAPTER ELEVEN

The Forensic Department of the Birton Force occupied the top of a new building in Bridge Street. There was a separate entrance round the back, through a tunnel, and a large freight lift big enough to take a stretcher on wheels. Aveyard parked his car in the small court beyond the tunnel, and pressed the buzzer for the passenger lift. When it arrived the police constable ran it straight to the sixth floor without asking. Aveyard didn't speak to him, walked along the corridor to a large double door at the end. He opened the double door, stepped inside. There was another set of double doors immediately ahead of him but he waited while the blast of air swirled all around him in the air-lock, scrubbing the outside of his clothing free of superficial dust. When the green light came on, the inner door clicked open, and he went through into the laboratory. Sergeant Bruton was waiting with Doctor Samson, and the Pathologist, Mr Bage.

"I thought you were going to bed?" he asked Dr Samson.

"I had a couple of hours. At my age, that's enough to restore the tissues. Can you bear to look at what we've got?"

"Is it bad ...?"

"It's interesting, Mr Bage thinks."

Mr Bage nodded his head, the complete boffin. Immaculate white coat, long thin fingers that looked as if they'd spent a lifetime immersed in Lysol. He was wearing horn-rimmed spectacles, and couldn't have been more than thirty-five years old.

The back bench of the laboratory was covered in opaque white glass. On the glass top were a number of 'specimens'. On the steel table in the centre of the room was a figure covered by a pale green sheet; Aveyard couldn't suppress a shudder as he walked past it. Mr Bage stood in front of the first specimen on the opaque white table, Aveyard one side,

Sergeant Bruton the other. In his hand he held a stainless steel scalpel with a razor's edge. "This is the first specimen," he said, his voice apologetic, as if conscious of the great burden of knowledge it must expose. "From this and our general examination of the genitals, we learn the subject was a male approximately sixty years of age. By comparing the size of certain bones with a standard scale of average sizes, we could estimate, and it's no more than an estimate, that the subject would be approximately five feet and ten inches, and would weigh approximately one hundred and sixty pounds."

"So Latham wasn't far out with his barley bag ..." Aveyard said to Bruton. Mr Bage waited courteously in case the Sergeant wished to reply. When no reply was forthcoming, he moved on to the next specimen, concealed beneath a cloth of white muslin. "This may be a shock to you," he warned them. Aveyard looked at Bruton behind the doctor's back. Bruton already was looking sick. "I have a reason for suggesting you look," Mr Bage said, "or I could just give you the information in a written report with a drawing, if you'd prefer ...?"

"Let's have a look," Aveyard said. Mr Bage carefully folded back the white muslin. Beneath it were two hands, severed at the wrist. The skin on one hand had been neatly peeled down to the wrist, exposing blood red tissue. Aveyard felt his stomach start to cartwheel. He looked away. Bruton was also looking away! Then he turned back.

"Sorry, it's rather gruesome," Mr Bage said.

"It's a bit of a shock, that's all."

"You'd be surprised how many women spend hours chopping stewing steak for the pot then faint at the sight of a small human cut ... Now, this is what I want you to look at." He handed Aveyard a large magnifying glass. "Look at the hand on the left," he said. Aveyard bent forward, held the glass midway between his eye and the hand on the table, then moved the glass up and down until the tissue of the hand came into perfect focus. Though the hand had been exposed to the flames and the surface was covered with charred skin, soot and wood ash, each line stood out with clarity. All along the lines, however, were tiny black circles, like the holes from which hairs have been plucked. Aveyard had never seen such a pattern

74

of holes before, though he had seen human flesh and skin magnified many times. He handed the glass to Sergeant Bruton, and moved aside to let him examine the hand. Now that he had become interested, the objects on the table seemed less gruesome to him, less obscene, and when his turn came to examine the hand on the right, he was able to do so without a trace of nausea. Once again, the magnification was such that he could see each grain of flesh, and scattered throughout, at random were these black dots, that appeared like holes in the other hand, but now revealed themselves as bristles embedded in the flesh. Whoever heard of a man with hair in the palms of his hand? Yet the black dots looked like the ends of hairs, projecting a thousandth of an inch from the flesh.

He handed the magnifying glass to Mr Bage. "You've seen what I mean," the pathologist said. Aveyard nodded. He knew he would explain and as yet there was no point in asking questions. They moved along the bench. Here a projection epidiascope had been mounted. On its bed on a glass plate was a thin sliver of flesh. Mr Bage switched on the light and an image was thrown onto a screen on the wall. It showed a bright red picture, and what looked like a pin or a straight hair. "This is a cross section of the flesh," Mr Bage explained, "and in it you can clearly see the spines whose ends you noticed with the aid of the magnifying glass. The hands of the subject have been impregnated with literally hundreds of these spines, like needle points."

"Do you know what the 'spines' are?"

"Not yet. We know what they are *not*, if that helps. Obviously they're not human hairs. They're not any sort of bones, fish bones, anything with a bone structure. The composition of them is entirely vegetable, and here's another thing, they were all impressed at a similar angle!" Mr Bage shut off the epidiascope, turned and placed his back to the bench.

"I've talked it over with Mr Bage," Dr Samson said, "and for what it's worth we've come to a conclusion."

"Hardly a conclusion," the pathologist interrupted, "more of a speculation. I wouldn't like to be questioned about this on oath."

"I'd be pleased to hear an informed guess, and would respect
75

it as such," Aveyard said.

Mr Bage waved his hand deferentially to Dr Samson, who cleared his throat before he spoke. "Please understand we've been doing a lot of guess-work. One thing we don't yet know is the actual cause of death. We know it wasn't a bullet, a knife, or strangulation. At the moment we're inclined towards 'death by natural causes'. The subject was obese, that much we can say for certain. His heart was surrounded by an excessive amount of fatty tissue. He's obviously been a man who's taken no exercise whatsoever, and though he weighed the amount of a strong muscular man, he should have weighed at least three stone less in view of his bone size and body structure. Certainly we've been able to find no evidence of a blow and think you can rule out any 'assault with a blunt instrument'. There's no evidence, and we've taken many X-rays and samples." Despite himself, Aveyard shuddered, thinking of these two doctors spending the night slicing small amounts of tissue from the cadaver, and examining them on an epidiascope.

"What about the spines in his hands?"

"Yes, I was just coming to that." Dr Samson looked about the laboratory; a pillar six inches round painted green stretched from floor to ceiling. "Come over here," he said. When they were all standing round, watching him, he stood about twelve inches from the pillar. "You understand that, at this stage, this is all supposition. Imagine our subject standing, just as I am standing, when the thing happens to cause his death. For the moment, let's say he had a heart attack. He starts to fall down ..." Dr Samson suited deeds to words, and bent his knees. His hands went forward instinctively to counterbalance his body weight. His hands reached the pillar, then clasped it. His body fell downwards, his hands rasped down the pillar.

"That's what we think happened," he said, when he stood up again.

"But what was that thing," Aveyard said, pointing to the pillar, "the thing he grabbed on his way down ...?"

Mr Bage looked at Dr Samson. "We think it was a plant," he said.

"A cactus?" Sergeant Bruton asked.

"A tall, spine bearing plant."

"Find that," Dr Samson said, "and you'll find where the man strapped into the Guy was standing at the moment of his death!"

# CHAPTER TWELVE

The Leeds Criminal Records Office acted quickly, and at half past two the Criminal Records clerk from the Birton Office brought several sheets of teleprinter to the Incidents Room in the village school. "I've held on to a copy for records," he said, "so you can keep these."

Stanley Robinson was an American citizen in 1945 when the war in Europe ended, a GI stationed at Yeadon in Yorkshire. He took his service discharge in England, since the girl he was courting refused to go to America on account of sick parents. He was married in Settle, in Yorkshire. Two years after marriage, his wife was discovered dead in bed. He had taken a job as a long distance night lorry driver, and it was suspected an intruder had broken into their home. However, the police investigation revealed his lorry had stood all night at the back of a transport café on Blubberhouses Moor, and though Stanley Robinson claimed he'd spent all night asleep in the cab, it would have been possible for him to return home, kill his wife, and get back to the lorry. It took the jury at Leeds Assizes six hours to reach a verdict of 'not guilty'. A contributing factor in their indecision, no doubt, was the life insurance policy Stanley Robinson had taken out on his wife. Her death gave him two thousand pounds.

With the money, he bought a small green-grocery in Golcar, near Pole House Moor, and the business prospered. Two years after his first wife died he married Elsie Clough from Golcar where no-one knew of his previous history, and two years later Elsie mistakenly drank a glass of bleaching liquor no doubt believing it to be her favourite dandelion-and-burdock. Stanley Robinson was in his shop at the time, but his fingerprints were found on the glass. The case against him looked bad but after a lengthy retirement, the jury at the Assizes found him not guilty; in Scottish Law the decision would have been 'Not Proven', a verdict which permits a jury to say in effect, 'Though we believe the suspect did it, the prosecution hasn't proved its case'.

Elsie Clough's father, a moderately rich wool-buyer, settled a thousand pounds on her when she married and bought them a two thousand pound house as a wedding present, next door to, and connected with the green-grocery business. Stanley Robinson walked away from that house and business, leaving everything inside it just as it had been when the police came to arrest him. Elsie Clough also had been insured, but this time for five thousand pounds.

Superintendent Aveyard had beckoned to Sergeant Bruton when he received the teleprint; the Sergeant read each page as Aveyard finished it. The last page contained four lines and was headed Other Interests. Stanley Robinson, apparently, had a good singing voice and had sung with the Colne Valley Male Voice Choir. He was also a member of the local branch of the Men of Trees, and the secretary of a group he himself had started, the Golcar Succulent Society.

## CHAPTER THIRTEEN

Aubrey Bollard was twenty-five years old and he'd never had a woman. Half past two on a Saturday and not a single prospect in sight. Damn! Saturday night on his own! Jimmy Bollard, his brother, had a date all right, trust him, and he'd come crawling back home at half past two smelling of scent and sex.

"Lend us your bush jacket since you won't be going out to-night," Jimmy said after dinner. Cocky sod; he could make even the simplest request into a sneer.

"I might. go out, you never know, I might have a date, you're not the only one can get a bit o' fancy ...!"

His dad's hand crashed on the dinner table making the plates jump and rattle. "Stop that. I'll not have dirty talk at the table in front of your mother!"

Dirty talk. If he thought that was dirty, he ought to be lying in bed at half past two of a Sunday morning when Jimmy came home ... Every Saturday night Aubrey tried to get to sleep before his brother came in, but he could never manage it; half past two found him listening for the shuffle of Jimmy's feet on the bedroom steps, waiting eagerly for the recital to start. Disgusting wasn't it? Disgusting!

"What you doing this afternoon?" his father asked, when his sister Daphne and their mother had taken the plates to the sink to wash them.

"Nothing much; you got something on?"

"I was thinking about taking the van over to Colonel Melville's; three hunters for shoeing, and there's a Meet on Monday."

"Want me to come?"

"I thought I might take Jimmy ..." Jimmy's head lifted from the comic book he was reading. "Hold on, Dad, I've got things to do this afternoon."

"What sort of things ...?"

"Well, got to have a bath, haven't I. Can't go out on a Saturday stinking of horses, can I. Not where I'm going ..."

"Horses was good enough to me all my life, yes, and ..."

"My father and grandfather before me!" Jimmy chanted the sentence for him. He'd heard it all before. Aubrey may be happy working with old Dad week-in and week-out, but Jimmy wasn't having much more of it. Jimmy had ambitions ...

Tom Bollard had been the village blacksmith all his life. There never used to be less than twenty or thirty hunters at Ulton Hall, and Tom Bollard, his father and his grandfather, had been responsible for the feet of every one of 'em. Of course everything had changed. There weren't any horses left in Ulton since Young Mr Arthur shut down the stables. Most blacksmiths had gone out of business during the last twenty years. Tom Bollard had been lucky having a son in the business with him; they'd bought a van, equipped the back of it with a portable bellows and hearth, and now looked after all the horses for twenty miles' radius; since that neighbourhood included the Pytchley, the Woodland Pytchley, the Fernie, they were never still. Tom Bollard had also diversified his interests, and now carried an oxy-acetylene kit everywhere he went. Farm equipment, gates, anything made of metal all came within his competence. Meanwhile, in Ulton Forge, Aubrey adapted a design of his great grandfather's and they manufactured and sold the Ulton Fire Basket, a piece of wrought iron work that found customers all over England. When Jimmy pulled his weight they could finish three a week, in addition to all the repair work and shoeing.

Aubrey had always been fascinated by his father's work, and took naturally to it from the moment he left the village school at fifteen. A tall gangling boy, he grew up into a thick solid young man, with muscles on him that could lift the portable anvil into and out of the van with ease. His hair was dark and curly, cut close to his head but helmeted down the back of his neck in modern long style. He spent a lot of time on his hair, hoping it would someday add to his appeal to women. Jimmy, damn him, had long hair that sprouted all over his head like cornsilk, and had never been seen to run a comb

81

through it; "Why should I comb it?" he'd say to Aubrey with a leer, "acts on the birds like a magnet that hair does; they love to run their fingers through it!"

Aubrey had hands that could span a dinner plate, broken, split and burned by hot iron; Jimmy kept a pair of leather gloves in the forge, and constantly wore them, much to his Dad's annoyance. "There's something immoral about them hands of yours," his Dad used to say. But Jimmy smiled.

"You'll be coming to the barn-dance?" Aubrey asked him.

Jimmy looked up again from his comic. "You bloody crazy," he said, then, when his father's hand crashed down on the table, "all right, I'll wash my mouth out with soap," he chanted.

"What's wrong with the barn-dance?" his father demanded. As a parish councillor he was on the organising committee. "Do you good to have a bit of clean village fun for a change instead of them immoral discotheques you frequent."

Jimmy slapped his comic down on the table. "What do you know about discotheques?" he demanded. "When have you ever been in one? That's you all over, condemning something you know nothing about ..."

"I don't need to go in one to know what happens," his Dad said smugly. "Look at the reports in the local paper; see what happened in Cottingham. How many was it, a hundred skinheads fouling the footpaths and decent people's front gardens!"

"That was the layabouts from Corby they wouldn't let in."

"And Wellingborough, skinheads again, outside the youth club. People in fear and trembling ..."

"Oh come off it Dad, who writes the script for you? Fear and trembling ..."

"You don't deny they sell drugs in some discotheques ...? The day any one of the three of you brings drugs into this house I'll break your back for you ..."

"Look Dad, they've smoked pot in the lavatory of Buckingham Palace, if you believe all you read. Just because the joints are being passed around, it doesn't mean to say you have to smoke 'em ... Anyway, Aubrey, in answer to your question, no, I don't think I'm coming to the barn-dance. I've got a date and she's not the barn-dance type, if you see what I mean ..."

Aubrey did see, all too clearly. None of Jimmy's birds was the barn-dance type ... "What did you have in mind for this afternoon?" he said to his Dad.

"I brought that gate from the Hall this morning. I'd like to get it finished soon as I can. We don't get much work from the Hall these days, but I still don't like to keep him waiting."

"Bloody forelock-puller," Jimmy muttered, but fortunately Tom Bollard didn't hear him.

"Come on," Nancy Bollard said, breaking in on them, "clear off out of my kitchen if you've finished your dinners. Our Daphne's going to set my hair for me, for tonight!"

The smithy was attached to the cottage on the north side, with a yard in which horses had stood to be shod. On the far side of the yard was the long shed in which Tom Bollard kept his stocks of iron, long flat bars, rods, square sections. The smithy itself was at the back of the yard, with heavy doors that could be lifted off their runners. There were two heating forges, and a row of anvils, heavy metal tables for electric welding. The smithy, however, was dominated by the big fire in the centre with its draught hood that rose up through the roof, and the big blowing machine behind it, worked by electricity. That fire could blow a piece of inch bar to white heat in under a minute, ready for hammering on the anvil. On the side was the smaller forge, with a draught still provided by its original bellows, used for fashioning horse shoes. Between the two the gate from Ulton Hall had been placed on three trestles. It stood about eight feet high when erected, and four feet wide, and had been designed for the back of the Hall where the wall curled round the corner of the green. A hole had been cut in the wall in Tom Bollard's grandfather's time, and he had made the gate to measure. The gate had stood there ever since, work typical of his grandfather, representing a twining plant. Each stem of the plant started from an oval at the bottom of the gate, then twined upwards, with shoots twisting out at the sides of the main stems, and leaves curling from them. The vertical stems had been forged together by what looked like tendrils, and yet the whole pattern was symmetrical, both in the length and in the breadth.

Aubrey examined the leaves; his great-grandfather had even

83

tapped a network of veins in each, so painstakingly realistic
had his work been. One of the leaves had been shaped to act
as a handle, and operated a bolt that engaged in the metal
plate set into the stone of the wall. To repair it properly would
mean forging a whole new section of three leaves and tendrils,
and Tom Bollard was determined it would be done as carefully
as his grandfather had made the original. Tom's skill was not
as it used to be; though he was adequate for banging horse-
shoes into shape, the gate repair needed the younger boy's
delicate touch. Tom admitted it; he was not a proud man, but
even so, he was glad he wouldn't be around when his son was
doing the work.

Aubrey set to examining the break in greater detail; then
he took a saw, a chisel and hammer, and cut out the broken
piece. First he made a new leaf, an exact copy of the one his
great grandfather had made, working with the 'slow' fire,
delicately tapping the iron into shape, forging it exactly where
he wanted it to go. 'A piece of iron the wrong temperature
has a life of its own under your hammer,' his grandfather had
always said, and it was true. Get the iron just right and you
can coax it anywhere; too hot and it bends capriciously, too
cold and it remains obdurate and cracks. His grandfather had
always talked to his metal; a too hot, too pliant iron was 'like
a woman'—'stand up, you bitch you,' he'd say; too cold and
it was 'sullen' and needed all the hammerings you could give
it.

When the leaf was finished he took a piece of bar, heated it,
and drew it out. It moved well under the soft blows of the small
hammer. Reheat it a moment, not too long looking for the
colour that proclaims it malleable, then curl it round the stocks
slotted into the anvil top, tap here, tap there, until the metal
begins to look like the grasping tendril of a vine, and even, or
is that just his imagination, seems to reach out of its own
accord. Iron's a living thing if you respect it. He splayed the
end of the stem of his leaf, heated the vine tendril and the leaf
together, then tapped them until they were one piece of metal;
he bent the stem of the leaf over, reheated it, bent it again, and
there it was, a leaf on a stem of a vine, with a tendril curling
upwards to seek the sun. He cooled it in the trough of water,

held it up and turned it in his fingers, feeling that soft glow of pride that comes with craft. "I wish great grandad could see that," he said. Not for the praise, no, not for that. Just so great grandad would know what he'd taught had not been wasted. Some men plant a tree, some a way of life, a craft that holds from generation to generation. It'd please great grandad to realise that.

He made two more leaves and finished the gate by half past four; lifted it single handed on to the flat topped barrow since there was no sign of Jimmy, and wheeled it left from the forge down Church Street, between the wall of the Hall and the village green. On the way he saw the two Bragg boys playing scratch football on the green with Jenny Latham, but from the giggles it seemed to be more scratch than football; Richard Hopton came past with his satchel containing the milk money he'd collected. "Lend us a pound," Aubrey said, an old joke that needed no answer. Sophie and Betty Blatsoe walked across the green, hair done up in curlers for the barn-dance. "See you tonight," they called, and he nodded. Tonight he'd pin his hopes on Iris Latham. Just the right age of eighteen. Her sister Helen was better looking but too young at sixteen; Iris, well, she'd do very nicely if what Jimmy said about her was true. And if she didn't bring a fella!

He was day dreaming about Iris Latham so hard his flat-topped barrow caught Mr Newsome in the midriff. He reeled back against the wall, hand clutching his middle. "Oh, Mr Newsome," Aubrey called out as he dashed round the barrow, "I just didn't see you. You came out of the gateway so quick ..." Arthur Newsome couldn't speak. He stood erect, one hand resting on the barrow, gulping deeply to get his breath back. Aubrey was fussing about, not daring to touch Mr Newsome. "I'm that sorry!" he kept on saying. Finally, Mr Newsome was able to breathe again and held out his hand to touch the lad, so obviously worried and distressed.

"My own fault, lad; there's no need to fret yourself." He turned round to look at the gap in the wall. "I thought there was a gate there ..." he said, puzzled.

"There was. I've got it here on the barrow. I've been mending it ..."

85

"Was something wrong with it?"

"It was broken. Dodson give it ... I mean, Mr Bragg gave it to my father to mend. I'm from the forge, Mr Newsome, Mr Bollard's forge."

"I know where you're from, lad," Arthur Newsome said, "I'm not as blind as people seem to think!"

"No, Mr Newsome, I wasn't meaning to suggest ..."

"Let it be, lad!" Arthur Newsome looked at the gate lying flat on the barrow. "Where was it broken?" he asked.

Aubrey showed him the new piece he'd put in. He'd cellulosed the whole gate black, and the new section was indistinguishable from the old. "That's a fine piece of work," Arthur Newsome said. "It may surprise you to know, since you seem to think I notice nothing, young lad, that I remember your great grandfather making that. I always liked the way he made the leaves curl on it. It used to be painted green and gold when I was a young lad," he said.

"I think it should be again," Aubrey said, proud to have the workmanship acknowledged.

"Ah, yes, but where would we find a painter to do it, these days?" Arthur Newsome said wistfully.

"I'd be pleased to do it myself," Aubrey said, "I'd be very pleased to get that gate back, as it was originally, aye, and keep it that way. I'd gladly pay for the paint myself, too," he said. Arthur Newsome chuckled. "There's no need for that lad," he said, "I think we can find the money for a pot of paint or two ... and I'm much obliged to you ..." He seemed at a loss for words. "Anyway," he said, "that'll stop it rusting, and you won't have to mend it again ..."

"That gate hadn't rusted," Aubrey said, his brows knit together in anger. "Sheer vandalism, that was. That gate had been forced, with a bar! If I could get my hands on the devil who'd force a bit of work like that ..."

"Forced, was it? Now who could want to do a thing like that ...?"

# CHAPTER FOURTEEN

"There's a lot of stuff up here nobody knows nought about," she said. "Look there's this railway I bought for him in Birton all them years ago. See how he's looked after it. That's a train, that is, electric. Your Dad had that to pieces many a time, cleaning it, making it go, and then there's all these lines and the stations and everything. Look at this. Time and again he showed this to me. How he made it work, but you put this mail-bag on the side here, you just hang it here like this, and then, when the train comes along this carriage hooks the mail-bag off the post just like it was real. It *was* real to your Dad. He used to make many a voyage on this. I used to get the lines for him, a bit at a time, when I could, and bring 'em home in my bag so's nobody'd know what I'd got there, and he used to add to it, add to it all the time there on the floor, and this line here used to go to Great Yarmouth, oh, he was always one for Great Yarmouth was your Dad, and a branch line going up as far as Scratby. It's all here in the books how he used to do it, and you can learn."

"Hours of fun he used to have with that railway did your Dad; and then he had all these plants to make his indoor garden, and always messing about with his plants. We keep the fire on all through the winter so's the plants don't get a chill. I wrote away for them, for him. And I'll write away for you, if you'll tell me, only tell me what you need."

"Oh there's many a time we've gone to Great Yarmouth, him and me, and changed trains and gone through to Scratby; I've never been there, but he used to describe it to me as real as could be because once in the early days he was stationed there in the Army and he used to tell me all about the lovely sand they had there, and going into Yarmouth. We used to bring the plants and put them alongside the line. 'Look,' he'd say, pretend you're in the carriage, riding first class, and you look out of the window and what can you see? Look ...?' and I'd look and I'd see the plants growing and he'd tell me the names of them all. That's a Solomon's Seal, that is, and that's the Pheasant's Eye. Can you see the Pheasant's Eye looking at you? Oh, he knew the names of 'em all right, and where they come from. All over the world. China and Japan, would you believe some of 'em come from, and Arizona and Mexico, and the Canary Islands, and even Jerusalem, they come from. He could travel the world, looking out through the windows of his train, at the plants. 'Where are we now,' he'd say, all excited, 'where are we now, Ma?' and I'd guess and say, 'Arizona, in the desert?' and he'd say, 'don't be so daft, that's Canariensis from the Canary Islands ... what would that be doing in Arizona!' And it can be the same for you, only you'll have to tell me what you want. You only have to tell me, that's all. Oh you're better off here; the world out there's a horrible place, and you're better off away from it, just like your Dad was, better off. And don't go doing what he did, though he only did it the once, but he was sorry about that every time it come back to his mind, when he went running off. But he come back sharp enough. Still it's turned out a good thing, hasn't it, when you think about it. There's bad things out there, bad things, and you're better off here with the train and the flowers and the plants. See the way he'd got all different kinds of leaf; you wouldn't think there was so many kinds of leaf would you, but he took such an interest. And I've enough to look after you, I mean I've enough coming in and put by to look after you and anything you set your heart on you can have because I can get it for you from Birton any time you ask. But you've just got to let me know what it is you want."

"There's bad things out there, and bad people, and I can't hardly say what they'd do to you, but it'd be something bad, you mark my words, because that's the way they are!"

"But you'll be all right here. I'll look after you. Anything you want. You've only got to tell me what it is ..."

## CHAPTER FIFTEEN

Helen Robinson was lying in a bed in the Intensive Care Unit at Birton Hospital. All the specialists and consultants had been to see her but there was little anyone could do. Arsenic in that quantity destroys so much body tissue and affects the metabolism in too many different ways. But at least they had established the exact cause of her trouble; a hypodermic syringe was used to inject two cubic centimetres of arsenic salt into the lumbar area. Her spine was paralysed and no-one could say for certain that, even if she lived, she'd ever walk again. Certainly her brain was affected, since the lumbar and the brain cells are in direct contact via the spine.

The Sister of the Intensive Care Unit was small and Irish; the specialists detested her. Fussy and overbearing, she made routine a misery, and many would have preferred to take patients elsewhere. 'What can we do, she's been with the hospital for donkey's years and she's efficient'. Dedicated to her job, she worked each evening, even when she was supposed to be off duty, until nine and ten o'clock. But to all the nursing staff who were obliged to work under her, she was a pain in the neck, and to the patients, often fighting for life after serious operations, her harsh and hectoring voice echoing through the corridor that abutted the small wards, was an additional burden many found almost insupportable.

"I can't see what good you're doing there!" she said to the woman Police Inspector sitting beside Helen Robinson's bed. "You're only getting in everybody's way! It's not right having the police loitering about in one of my wards."

"Shut up, Sister," the specialist checking the patient's pulse rate said, "and get about your business!"

The Sister, mortally offended for the tenth time that day, flounced out of the ward. Her voice could be heard in the cor-

89

ridor like a tinsmith's rasp, chivvying a junior nurse, exacting her narrow-minded revenge.

The specialist finished his examination. "She's a tartar," he said to the Inspector, "but in this case I'm inclined to agree. There is very little point to your being here, since I'm afraid the chances of this patient ever speaking again are very small!"

Stanley Robinson was 'helping with enquiries', sitting in the basement 'waiting room' at police headquarters. Though comfortably furnished with armchairs and a carpet, the room had no window and a self-locking door. A police constable sat in a corner of the room at a desk; he appeared to be copying names from a long list but in no hurry to complete the job; his purpose was to watch every move Stanley Robinson made. Dinner had been served to both of them; meat pie, cabbage, and instant potatoes, rhubarb tart to follow though the rhubarb was tinned, and the tea with which they washed it all down was stewed. The Constable apologised but Stanley laughed; "If you had to eat some of the muck they turn out in our works canteen," he said, "you'd think this was Claridges ..."

The prisoner would obviously like to chat to relieve the boredom of waiting, but the constable had had his orders.

It was about five o'clock when Superintendent Aveyard and Sergeant Bruton arrived. Aveyard beckoned and the constable left the room. The Sergeant was carrying a plant pot wrapped in paper. He stood the pot on the table, unwrapped the paper and stood back. Aveyard, and Stanley Robinson both looked at the plant the pot contained. It was like nothing Aveyard had ever seen before this day. Pale green, it stood twenty-two inches high (the Sergeant had measured it) and was four and a quarter inches in diameter at the widest point, a long upright pillar of a plant, with spines sticking out of it in neat vertical rows. There were over twenty separate rows like stripes running up and down the plant; each row consisted of thousands of fine hairs, interspersed with stronger needles about a half an inch long.

"That's my Cleistocactus Straussii," Stanley said, "you ought to know better than to bring it out of doors in November!"

"It looks as if it's been damaged," Aveyard said, pointing at one vertical row of spines which appeared to be bent downwards. Several spines had been broken away from the plant and were hanging trapped in the white fuzz of fine hairs. He turned the pot round; the other side seemed to be damaged in the same way.

"Yes, it's a damned shame," Stanley Robinson said, "if it hadn't been for that I'd have taken a First at Birton Show last week!"

"For an American you speak remarkable English," Aveyard said suddenly.

"Whadya want—I should talk this way?" Stanley Robinson said, his voice thick and nasal.

"All right, I take the point—you're bilingual," Aveyard said wrily, "now about the cactus plant ... You wouldn't like to tell us how it was damaged, and when."

"I didn't know you were interested in Succulents?"

"You'd be surprised at what interests the Sergeant and me."

"Daftest thing you ever heard. It was standing on the lower staging. I'd climbed up to the plank, you must have seen it in my greenhouse where I keep a few pots. I grabbed a pot with one hand, started to climb down. The pot was turned upside down, and I hadn't noticed, but there must have been a crack right round the base of the pot. The top dropped off, and I was left holding the base in my hand. The top, a ring of pot, d'you see, fell down, dropped neat as a hoopla round my Cleistocactus. It took me ten minutes to get it back off the plant, but I couldn't do anything about the damage it'd done, falling down."

Aveyard looked at the Sergeant whose face he could read like an open book. 'Pull the other one, it has bells on,' the Sergeant's look seemed to say. Plausible fellow, this Robinson. Have to be to appear in court twice on a murder charge and get away with it.

"I wish you hadn't brought it out of the greenhouse," he said, "in November!"

Mr Bage was annoyed! It took him thirty seconds. One needle from the corpse, one from Robinson's cactus, both side by side on the epidiascope.

"Not the same at all," he said, "the one from the body is

brown in substance, this one is white. You've probably killed that beautiful plant bringing it out of the greenhouse in November. You should have left it where it was; I could have photographed it *in situ*, could have told you immediately it wasn't what we're looking for. No, if it's a Cleistocactus at all, which I doubt, it'll be a Jujuyensis, or a Tupizensis!"

"I quite agree," Aveyard said, "now that you come to mention it!" Mr Bage took off his glasses and looked at him through pale eyes.

"We keep telling you people," he said heavily, "to leave things alone! Leave everything alone until someone from forensic has seen and photographed it, *in situ*. That's not so difficult, is it? Yet you love to come dashing in here waving whatever it is you've found like a piece of treasure trove, and then expect us to say what a good little boy you've been! You've probably murdered this plant, and all for nothing!"

# CHAPTER SIXTEEN

Sergeant Jim Bruton always read the *Evening Telegraph*. "It should be made compulsory reading for policemen," he said, "you never know when a name might jump out at you if you're alert. Last week, James Machonochie, apprehended in Corby for stealing a bicycle. Most people would ask why steal a bicycle. I wondered, why Corby. Jimmy lives in Rushden, not Corby! He's a sneak-thief, our Jimmy! Sure enough the following morning the Corby report showed a rash of sneak-thefts. Jimmy would have got away with stealing a bike, two pounds and don't be a naughty boy but one phone call and he's gone away for two years ..."

"Very commendable!" Aveyard said sourly, "but what's that got to do with bodies on bonfires, and a girl with a dose of arsenic in her spine ...?"

"You should read the *Evening Telegraph*. Reports of local Societies; they're all there! Horticulture Shows, Cactus Societies; one name keeps cropping up ... Collis. Perhaps we should pay Mr and Mrs Collis a visit, do our homework!"

"Green fingers Bruton, they'll be calling you next," Bill Aveyard said. "You're not just a pretty face!"

Collis's shop stands in a row next to a television and radio shop and the Finedon Post Office. Outside are old orange boxes with planks between them; on the planks in season stand boxes of fruit and vegetables, potted plants with exotic blooms, fuchsias, gloxinias, beloperone guttata the locals call 'the shrimp plant'. In the shop sheaves of cut flowers stand ready to start a slow death in a vase on a sideboard, remembering a birthday or an anniversary, or the fact someone snarled a bit the previous evening coming tired from the shoe factory. Some women charm easy when you carry a spray of gladioli ...

Mr Collis is a tall man, though years of bending over cactus seeds have given him a kindly stoop; he wears a grey shop coat and has a slow easy smile for customers who'd rather shell fresh peas than boil a bit of life back into the frozen stuff. Mrs Collis works in the shop beside him, jotting the price of purchases on a scrap of paper, a used sugar bag, adding 'em up, and sometimes doing what no cash register has the heart to do, knocking the pennies off the total for a pensioner, or a deserving customer. It's that kind of shop; you get the feeling theirs is an honest business of supplying your demands, not extracting every last bit of 'purchasing power' from you.

Aveyard waited in the shop until a woman had concluded a purchase of two pounds of early sprouts before introducing himself and his Sergeant. "You'd better come through," Mrs Collis said, leading the way into a tiny sitting room behind the shop, an Aladdin's cave of silver cups and trophies awarded at horticultural shows up and down the country. There were pictures of cacti on the walls, books of cacti in a book-case in the corner of the room. "They tell me you know a thing or two about cacti," Aveyard said by way of introduction.

"We've been doing it long enough," Mrs Collis said modestly. She sat in a cretonne covered armchair, at ease and prepared for questions. Sergeant Bruton sat in the other armchair, his ever present notebook out, his pencil poised. Superintendent Aveyard seated himself on a hard-backed chair. "It's hard to know where to start," he said. "We've discovered a body in a village near here ..."

"Ulton," she said. "Yes, I've heard. Found on the Bonfire, wasn't it ...?"

"News travels fast ..."

"I was talking to someone we know in Ulton on the telephone last night ..."

"It wouldn't happen to be a Mr Robinson?" Aveyard asked. Shot in the dark, but why not ...?

"Yes, it was. How did you know?"

"He has a damaged cactus. He told me it'd been on a plank he keeps pots on. He reached up for a pot; the pot was cracked, and the top dropped like a ring, straight down his cactus. And that's what damaged the spines ..."

94

"It would, wouldn't it? He'd have taken a prize at Birton if it hadn't been damaged."

"And you think it's possible for the cactus to be damaged that way?"

Mrs Collis hesitated. "Oh yes, I should think so," she said. "It would break some of the spines off short; it wouldn't fetch them right out, you see, just sort of shave them off a bit, break the tops off ..."

Aveyard glanced at Sergeant Bruton. Now they were getting somewhere. Now for the sixty-four dollar question. "Would you get the same effect if a man rubbed down that plant, accidentally, with his open hands ...?"

Mrs Collis laughed. "You'd be surprised how many times that happens at shows," she said. "We always put a big notice there, saying, please do not touch, but you'd be amazed at the number of people who come by and say, isn't that a lovely thing, then rub their hands all the way down it!" She laughed again. "Keeps 'em busy with the tweezers for hours, that does!"

"Do the spines stick in ...?"

"Well, with a Cleistocactus you probably wouldn't get the whole spine. You'd get part of it. You see, it would break, because the spines are long and they're glassy; these glassy white spines that were brittle, well, they'd break off. You'd get part of the spine in, you see ..." She paused.

"Yes ..."

"But you wouldn't get the whole spine. It wouldn't come right out from the areole, from the centre ..."

"How long would the spine be? I mean, how much of the spine would go into his hand, do you think?"

"You could get quite a minute bit, or perhaps a quarter or a half of an inch, it just depends."

"So the size is right," Sergeant Bruton said, "but the colour is wrong ..." Mrs Collis looked from one to the other.

"You've found some spines, have you?"

Bruton looked at Aveyard. How much could they disclose? How fair was it to ask for information, without disclosing the uses to which that information might be put? "We've found spines in the hands of the victim of that sad affair in Ulton,"

Aveyard said, gravely.

"And you think he might be one of our members ... We'd have heard, if one of our members was dead like that, was missing."

"I don't necessarily think he was a cactus grower," Aveyard said, "we think he was standing near a cactus when he died ... I must ask you not to say anything about this," he said, seeing the disapproval in Bruton's eyes. Bruton believed police matter was sacred; 'we've got to take a chance', Aveyard's look implied.

"We found spines in the dead man's hands, but they're the wrong colour ..."

"Cleistocactus straussii would be white, well, clear, almost like glass ..."

"Yes, we've found that out, the hard way!" Aveyard said ruefully. "Can you think of any other plant we could look out for ...? Assuming a man fell," Aveyard said, "and reached out and clutched a cactus plant, and got spines in his hands ..."

"Well, one of the easiest, really one of the worst offenders is any of the opuntias. And they're quite common ..."

"Opuntias?" Aveyard said, to pronounce the word so that Bruton would have a chance to spell it correctly.

"Yes, the padded opuntias; any of the opuntias for that matter. Some are much worse than others because they've got the slightly barbed spine, some are very barbed; you can't see it with the naked eye ..."

"But you'd see it under a microscope ..."

"Oh yes, under a microscope ..."

"Like a fish hook?"

"Yes, like a fish hook. They're terrible things. You've only got to brush against one, hardly touch it, and you'll get a finger full, of the tiny ones especially ..."

"And the opuntia is a common plant?" Sergeant Bruton asked.

"Most people, especially beginners, they nearly always have at least one opuntia because it's one of the easiest to grow and it's the one most people think of as a cactus. They see it on the pictures, you know, cowboy pictures, Arizona, and now it's on the TV ..."

"Do you have one here?"

"Yes, we have one or two, though we're going out of 'em."

"Could we see it?" Aveyard asked, looking round.

What did he expect? A small greenhouse stuck at the back of the small house behind the shop, with a few dry looking cactus plants on a shelf. He'd seen cactus plants of course, but never could understand why people bothered to grow them, small, stunted, dangerous things, dust and fly traps mostly. He was totally unprepared when Mrs Collis took him and the Sergeant outside, into the greenhouses.

There were two greenhouses in the back garden, and each contained what looked like a thousand plants of all types. Certainly there were the small scrubby looking spiny cacti he had seen outside grocers' shops, but also many towering specimens in delicate shades of grey and green and brown, some covered in white hair that looked as if it had just been combed, others sporting red, yellow or white flowers which seemed to grow out of the solid flesh of the cactus itself. Some were five and six feet high, and many inches in diameter, with spines that projected as much as two or three inches; others were covered with a white down of tiny hairy spines which masked the sharp spines below. Arizona, Mexico, the heights of Bolivia and the Andes, all brought within these two small glass-houses in the heart of rural England. "We got that one from California," Mrs Collis said, "that one from Arizona, that one from South Africa." They'd scoured the world for specimen plants, many of a rich succulent beauty. "There's the one they call Euphorbia Splendens," Mrs Collins said, "and legend has it that was the plant used to make the Crown of Thorns they put on Jesus. This one," she said, pointing to a plant the size of a human head, "has this 'hair' growing on it that some people wash and comb before the exhibitions ..."

"Fancy ringing up the hairdresser, booking an appointment and then saying it's for your cactus ..." Aveyard murmured.

The opuntia was at the far end of the first greenhouse; it looked like three padded pillows of oval shape joined end to end.

Aveyard bent near the plant. Growing from the green surface of each of the 'pillows' was a pimple, and the spines grew

97

in that pimple, as many as fifteen each. "Those are the areoles," Mrs Collis said. "On a rose, or a Crown of Thorns, the spines grow out of the plant itself. They'd be inclined more to tear your hand if you grasped 'em hard. But these opuntia spines, in that areole, would break off and stick in, and then you'd have a wonderful time with the tweezers, getting 'em out again."

# CHAPTER SEVENTEEN

Tea-time Saturday, and Sergeant Bruton's standing in the centre of the kitchen of Stanley Robinson's house in Eastfields, a search warrant in his top pocket, but a look of utter amazement on his face.

"It has to be here somewhere," he says.

The 'scene of the crime' squad has been and gone. Everything's been examined and photographed with great care. Fingerprint powder on all the doors and door jambs, on the table, the shelves, the cupboard doors. Photographs of the kitchen general view, close-ups of anything unusual, *anything*, even a grease spot on the floor with a mark of a foot in it. That's an easy one; the sole print matches exactly the pair of shoes Helen Robinson was wearing. She's a careless housekeeper, half used tins of instant coffee with the lids left off so the coffee hardens, pans put away not properly cleaned, the grill of the stove filthy with grease, a stinking rag tucked behind the sink taps.

"It has to be here, somewhere," Sergeant Bruton says again.

A search team of three is sitting round the table, dejected, disgruntled. They're specialists; the leader of the group, Tom, is a man of about fifty, large, flabby, who moves like a cat. Tom has shifty eyes that flick constantly over the ground, in corners, round pictures. Nothing escapes the penetration of those eyes; the men who work with him swear he projects his own X-rays. It's a simple matter of possibilities. Here is a house in which a man and his wife have lived. It's a modern house so you can forget about secret rooms and trapdoors, bolt holes where priests hid from tyranny and torture. The man comes from his bed, downstairs, makes a pot of tea. He climbs the stairs again, hands his ever-loving a pot of tea, and goes out with his own pot to the greenhouse at the back. Nothing special in there; a few chrysanthemums in pots, a few plants lying on their sides, or plunged into a bed of ashes to mark time through the long winter. About twenty cacti and succulents on a table, a pan of earth, sack of peat and John Innes compost. The man sits drinking tea, looks at his plants dreaming of the horticultural delights he'll have, the prizes at shows, next year, the year after, when the seed has taken.

A man trundles an electric trolley from the dairy, milk bottles clanking to every door in the street. Nothing's different this morning except it's colder than it should be even for November, and Mrs Grainger from number seven has left a note in the bottle cutting her order to two pints instead of three. The milkman's not surprised; he saw the new curtains go up and knew they'd have to be paid for somehow; curtains for your windows, or calcium rich milk for your kids' bones? It's disgusting how often the windows win!

Bruton read the notes of his interrogation again. Nothing extraordinary this morning, nothing. "I walked to the door of the house the way I allus does, put down two pints, took two empty bottles, walked out again, saw nothing, heard nothing. The time was approximately five-forty ayem and I'm making this statement of my own free will!" Proper comic!

Bruton looked at the search squad. "It must be here somewhere," he said. They looked at each other. "We'll do it all again," he said, "but ..." Each one shook his head. Bruton flipped the page of his notebook. Harry Greaves, postmaster, shop-keeper, youth leader, lender of small sums of cash, sage and counsel. "The letters and a catalogue. I put the two letters through the box, the catalogue under a bottle of milk. They don't make letter boxes big enough these days ..."

"How did you know it was a catalogue?"

"Because on the envelope was printed, 'This is a catalogue'."

"When you push the letters through the box flap, do you ever look through into the house?"

"Whatever for? I'm not a peeping Tom, and I've certainly more to do than waste my time squinting through letter boxes to see if I can catch the missis in her knickers ..."

"Yes, I know you have. I'm sorry, I wasn't implying ..."

100

"If the injection took place before the milkman came," Tom said, "the hypodermic could have been stuck inside a milk bottle and carried away."

"The milkman would have seen it ..."

"Yes, I suppose he would!"

Minnie Barnes delivers the papers in Eastfields. "Pushed 'em through the letter box ..."

"You got 'em through easy ...?"

"No, I had to fold 'em. Well, I didn't push 'em through, if you know what I mean, just sort of stuck 'em there. I'm not supposed to; they play merry stink if I do that an' it rains. No, I didn't look through the windows. Too much of a 'urry ..."

The Sergeant closed his book. "Only two possibilities," he said, "either it's here somewhere, or whoever used it took it with him, or if Mr Robinson used it, he's chucked it as far away as it'd go ..."

"That makes three possibilities," Tom said.

One of the men picked up the box at his feet, held the probe towards a tea-spoon on the table and switched on. There was a clicking noise from the box, an adaption of a mine detector. It clicked any time it came near metal; it'd have sniffed out the needle of a hypodermic in any plant pot, bag of peat, compost, or buried in the soil of the garden. They'd found twenty or more nails, rusted hinges, pieces of metal, all buried in the ground; they'd examined every inch of floorboard and none had been recently replaced. The ground floors were all compound, hardened months ago. They'd looked in cupboards, drawers, wardrobes, behind the pelmets, in the cushions of chairs, down the sides of the arms where pennies and pins drop. The central heating boiler converted to North Sea gas wouldn't have melted a glass and steel syringe.

The Sergeant sat down in the armchair. "Funny place to put an armchair, in the kitchen," one of the search men said, for want of something better.

"An older man married to a younger girl," the Sergeant said, "I imagine he liked to sit comfortably to do up his boot-laces."

The Sergeant put his hand behind him. "This chair's damp," he said as he stood up. A small patch of damp at the bottom of the back of the chair, just above the cushion. No one spoke. Tom took the forked screwdriver out of his canvas satchel, and one by one prised loose the tacks holding the fabric to the chair. Beneath the fabric a canvas pad had been stitched to each of a half dozen coiled springs to give the back of the chair resilience.

"We got a click, but thought it was those damn springs," Tom said. Half way down, in the centre, a cradle of cotton had been tied inside a spring.

"Button thread," Sergeant Bruton said, "or builders' line."

They peeled the back from the chair, and the canvas covered pad. A hypodermic was lying in the bottom of the chair, needle pointing sideways. The plunger of the hypodermic was near the bottom of the barrel, two ccs gone, one cc remaining, dripping out through the needle point.

"See what he did," Tom said. "He took the back off the chair, fastened the hypodermic in the centre of that coil spring with thread. She sits in the chair and leans back. Her weight presses against the coil springs and they close ... The hypodermic isn't flexible, and can't go back, so the needle comes out through the fabric of the chair and sticks into her. Her extra weight forces the plunger forward and she gets two ccs in her back through the needle. She jerks forward off the needle and the coil spring pulls it back out of sight in the fabric. That's in theory. What actually happens is that the coil spring pulls the needle back all right but the thread cradle doesn't hold properly on the smooth barrel, and the hypodermic drops into the bottom of the back of the chair. We come along with our detector and think the reaction we get comes from the coiled springs you'll always find in an armchair."

Sergeant Bruton had picked up the hypodermic, holding its needle with a pair of tweezers. One of the men opened a small plastic bag, and Bruton was just about to put the hypodermic into it when suddenly he changed his mind and put it back into the chair.

"Is that where it was? Is that how it was lying?" he asked Tom. Tom nodded.

"Right, leave it there. I imagine Mr Bage will just have gone to bed after being up all night. Give him a ring, and tell him what we've found. He'll enjoy coming out here, to examine it *in situ*!"

# CHAPTER EIGHTEEN

When Tom Bollard returned from the shoeing, he stopped at Harry Greaves' shop. Harry had just locked the door. Tom pressed the buzzer and when Harry appeared, he held open the door of the Bedford van. Harry climbed in beside him and they drove to the Vicarage. Francis Elks was waiting for them, with Herbert Larrapin, and Bill Hopton.

"I'm sorry to ask you to come to this emergency," Francis Elks said, "but I feel there is a matter we should discuss. I know the barn-dance is all planned for tonight, and we've got in the extra supplies and everything, but I'm a little worried about the propriety of holding such a function with the shadow hanging over the village. After all, a man has died, in tragic circumstances. It wouldn't do for us to appear, well, how can I put it, callous ..."

The four men were silent, thinking. A winter's night was settling outside, the air cold. There were lights in the village street they could see through the Vicarage windows. People walking out there, returning home from Saturday afternoon shopping in Birton, through a November smell of wet leaves.

Tom Bollard spoke slowly, "Of course, we're all upset by what's happened ... I think I speak for everybody when I say that ..."

Each of then nodded a silent affirmation.

"... and though we're all very upset, I mean the Robinson business is a real shaker and no mistake, we've got to think of the young 'uns. Which is better, to have 'em sitting at home brooding, or run the barn-dance as planned so they can forget about it all ..."

"Nobody wants to seem callous," Larrapin said, "I've had all the reporters in the pub and it'll appear in all the newspapers but, though I don't think we should forget it, there's a case to be made for putting it out of mind. At least for this evening!"

"But what happens," Bill Hopton said, "if some reporter takes a picture of the barn-dance under one of those headlines, you know, village enjoys itself while police look for murderers ...?"

"They seem to have arrested Stanley Robinson," Francis Elks said ...

How do you live your life—moment to moment, or thinking solely about long term effects? The kids had been looking forward to the barn-dance; they could do nothing about the murders so why penalise them? The discussion went backwards and forwards between the men, should we do what we think is right or behave the way people expect ...? Will cancelling the barn-dance impede the investigation? Who could say? They went groping among instincts, just as the police themselves were groping in the macabre world of a man who'd set another on the top of a bonfire.

When they took the vote, Greaves, Bollard, the Vicar and Larrapin were all in favour of the barn-dance continuing. Hopton was against it.

"One thing is certain," he said, "you'll be well advised to keep a guard on the doors of the Church room, and let nobody in but people we all know, from the village. Otherwise, you'll have the place full of gawpers!"

"Shall you be one of the guards?" Harry Greaves asked Bill Hopton, seeking by involving him to take the sting out of the vote. "No," he said, "I shan't be coming to the barn-dance. If anybody wants me, they'll find me either at home, or in the Church!"

"You'd better say a prayer for Bert Dunkley," Herbert Larrapin said, "wherever that poor soul might be!"

# CHAPTER NINETEEN

Amy Dunkley put on her winter coat and came out of their cottage leaving Fred Dunkley inside, dozing by the Raeburn. She turned left after some indecision, then began down Church Street. As she walked along she looked in each gateway she passed, behind every hedge. It was a bitter November night, but she didn't feel the cold on her person. Her eyes darted this way, that way, still looking as she had been looking all day and all the previous night. Already the clear moon was quite high and cast steely shadows from every tree, every hedgerow; the paths were dry and there was no dew yet; later, she knew, the heavy cold wet blanket would settle on everything, she could imagine her boy, somewhere out there, shivering beneath a hedgerow. All her mental pictures of him were shivering beneath a hedgerow. Time and again Fred had told her the boy would be in a barn somewhere, wrapped in sacks beneath the hay. He'd be warm as could be. "There are men who live that way," he told her, "tramping from place to place, sleeping in barns among hay, a night here, a night there." But she couldn't comprehend what he was saying. Her boy was out there, out there somewhere, beneath a hedgerow, shivering from cold, hunger, lack of love and frightened. No clouds in the clear heavy blue November sky, and a bright moon that offered no warmth, not even the warmth of amber light. The moonlight was blue and cold, stark and sheer, casting brittle edged shadows. Amy was crying and calling Bert's name quietly but continuously to identify herself. Fred had told her Bert would have found a pair of trousers somewhere; "people leave work trousers in barns," he said, "he's bound to have found an old pair of trousers to put on, an old jacket, a woollen pullover to keep hissen warm ..."

"I thought you said the hay'd keep him warm?"

There were sheds at the end of Church Street, old barns that had been used when Church Farm had been worked independently instead of being incorporated into East Lodge Farm. Three barns; one an open Dutch barn full of hay, sweet smelling winter keep for Hopton's herd of Guernseys. The sides of the stack were straight and sheer, but Amy scrabbled them to one side of the iron roof support and climbed up in the angle. Four or five bales had been removed in the centre of the stack making a shallow cave. She dropped down into the cave, sniffing, feeling about in the semi-dark. A bale of hay had been spread out over the floor of this cave, a good foot thick. Had somebody been there? Had they spread the straw out for a blanket? She stood in the cave of hay, willing herself to accept any knowledge it might give her, but after a few minutes, she climbed out again, confident that, if Bert had spent time there, she must have known.

One of the other two barns was empty.

The third barn appeared to be padlocked; but when on impulse she touched the hasp, she found it had been forced. She stood there for a moment, listening. How easy to deceive oneself; how easy to imagine something happens because you wish it desperately. She thought she could hear, through the closed door, the rustle of someone inside. "Bert!" she said, her voice no more than a whisper. The rustle didn't stop. She folded back the forced hasp then opened the door.

The rustle stopped.

"Bert, love," she said, "it's me!"

Silence inside the barn. Absolute silence.

Amy Dunkley held up her torch, then switched it on. Half the barn filled by a threshing machine; the other half held hay. The front of the hay stack had been pulled down and spread on the ground. She gasped, and switched off the torch, turning to run out of the barn, sobbing with disappointment. "Your boy Bert's not here, Mrs Dunkley," she heard Sam Tewson call after her. Helen Latham was giggling uncontrollably.

Amy Dunkley ran down the lane, sobbing, until she was out of breath and had to stop. There was no room in her mind for the scene she had just witnessed. "Where is my Bert, where *is*

107

he?" was all she could think. For the hundredth time she cursed Olive Abbott for frightening him. Fancy using a word like 'sacrilege' to a young boy! The police would have given him a good talking to, but that would have been the end of it. She'd asked that nice young Superintendent; there was no chance of a charge being made if the Rector didn't want it. And then, even if a charge had been made, they wouldn't have prosecuted, the Superintendent had said. It would have been up to the Chief Constable to decide, of course, but they'd have given the boy an official reprimand without him ever appearing before juvenile courts. Bert didn't know this, and if he'd been hiding in the hay when they came to look for him, he'd have burrowed down deeper. Poor mite. "Bert," she called softly, "Bert, it's me, it's your mother ..."

There was no reply though she stood still, listening.

In the field beyond the stacks a cow was mooing sadly, quietly. She went to the gate and in the dark several of the cows came to her, expecting food. Amy looked across the field at the lights of Ulton in the half-distance. The cow mooed again, then pushed its muzzle under Amy's hand hanging over the gate. Amy stroked the cow's muzzle, feeling the soft skin beneath her hand, smooth as a baby's, remembering the touch. "Oh Bert," she cried, "where are you, where are you, where *are* you ...?"

Olive Abbott was sitting by her fire, embroidering a pillow case.

"If he comes here," Amy Dunkley said, "bring him down home right away, won't you ...?"

"He'd be hungry if he'd been hiding out ..."

"I know he would, that's why I'm saying, bring him down home right away, don't make him a meal and keep him here ..."

"Why should I do a thing like that?" In and out with the needle, her speed the only signs of anger. No, come to think of it, not anger at eighty-seven. You don't have anger at that age; you don't have feelings some would say, at that age, but they'd be wrong. "It's not right," Olive said, "bringing the police to a lad as young as our Bert; harsh as oats ears that is, and quite un-called for. When I was a young girl dads commanded respect from their lads."

"It's not Fred's fault ..."

"Then whose fault is it? Poor innocent mite, and setting the police on him like he was a mad dog ..." She dug her needle deftly into the cloth, put the cloth on the table beside her, then smoothed the dress she wore over her knees. She stood up, and reached to get a lump of coal from the bucket beside the fireplace. "Here, let me do that," Amy said, but Olive brushed her to one side. "I can manage," she said, "I can manage." She took a chunk of coal from the bucket and put it on the fire without using the tongs. "One of these days you'll burn yourself," Amy warned her. Olive laughed, wiped her hand on the cloth she kept hanging over the rim of the bucket. With no oils left in her old skin, the coal dust didn't cling.

Olive's tea was still laid on the table. "Shall I clear the table for you and wash up before I go?" Amy asked.

"Leave it, leave it," Olive said, fiercely independent, and determined not to be helped. She'd not forgotten the events of the previous evening, or so it seemed; letting Amy clear the table would have been a sign of her forgiveness. Bread and butter, thinly sliced, a pot of strawberry jam, and a packet of digestive biscuits, chocolate on one side, stood on the table-top.

"If our Bert comes in here before he comes home," Amy said, relenting, "you can give him one of them chocolate digestives before you bring him. He loves 'em!"

Olive smiled at her. She sat back in her chair, picked up her embroidery. "I see they're going ahead with the barn-dance then," she said. "One in the flames, one in the coffin, one in the prison shedding tears as'll never dry. Aye, and there's another one somewhere as is glad it's all over, and him to sleep at nights now, if his current fancy'll let him. A baby as was made and never born, and perhaps was never meant to live; it's happened before, I've seen it all before. A pool of water's still, but there's movement below; a dog lies dead but there's maggits under the skin, eggs laid by fat-fed blue boys that grows in times of waste and plenty ..."

\* \* \*

"Olive's taking it hard," Amy said to Fred when she got home. "She was talking to herself when I left."

"I'm afraid something will have to be done about the old girl one of these days. Pity she hasn't any relatives left alive to look after her. Still, you've got to admit, she has her prophetic moments, our Olive. She'd have made a grand fortune teller, dress her up in a black skirt with the signs of the Zodiac and a funny hat ..."

"Fred, how can you ..."

"How about us going to the barn-dance? You and me? How about it?"

Amy drew from him in horror. "Oh, I know what you're going to say," he said, "with our young Bert missing an' all; but look, lovey, what can we do about it? We've worn ourselves to the bone looking for him, and as far as I'm concerned he's nowhere to be found. Wherever he is, he's found clothes and food, and the little bugger's doing all right for himself, probably laughing at us knowing how worried we are."

"Or else he's lying somewhere, dead, haven't you thought of that, you hard-hearted devil, haven't you thought of that then ...?"

He gripped her arms. "He's not dead," he said, "or the police would have found him and told us. He's missing, but it's my bet he's found himself a nice billet somewhere, and he's laughing his bloody head off ... where are you going ...?"

She'd broken from his grasp and had grabbed her coat. "I'm going out," she said. "I won't stay in the house with you another minute!" Helpless he watched as she opened the door, went out and banged it behind herself. He stood there for a moment then picked up the evening paper and sat down in his chair by the stove. The events of the Bonfire were on the front page with a picture of the smouldering pyre and a photograph of Superintendent Aveyard. The 'arsenic poisoning' started on the front page but overlapped to the back page. It was a piece of masterly writing, told everything but said nothing, other than that Stanley Robinson was 'helping with enquiries'. Boy reported Missing, page four, last column, low down. They'd printed the muzzy photograph Amy had given them despite Fred's protest it no longer looked like the boy.

Somebody with a Wellingborough address had a greenhouse for sale, eight by six, purchaser to dismantle. Just the size Fred was looking for, second-hand. He ringed the column in which the advert appeared.

Helen Robinson died at three fifteen p.m. on Saturday the sixth of November, without ever recovering consciousness. The autopsy, which Mr Bage carried out immediately, confirmed that death was due to the administration of twenty milligrams of arsenic in aqueous solution, but also that Helen Robinson at the time of her death was pregnant. Mr Bage took a sample of the unborn baby's blood.

# CHAPTER TWENTY

Bored with the clatter of typewriters in the Incidents Room, the cigarette smoke, the fug, and the vending machine coffee, Aveyard and Bruton took an hour off and drove to Aveyard's flat. The time was half past six. "Your wife will be wondering where you are," Aveyard said.

"She's used to it."

"You're a very lucky man!"

"I know!"

"I've just had an idea," Bill Aveyard said, "Does your wife like going out?"

"Sometimes. We don't get much opportunity, as you know!"

"Why not take her out tonight ...?"

"You wouldn't be thinking of a certain barn-dance?"

"How is your dancing?"

"Rusty?"

"You'll be all right. They have a caller, you know, shouts out the steps ..."

"That's a throw-back!"

"One of the good things about village life. One week a disco-theque at the youth club, run by the Vicar, with a group, next week a folk-dance, then a barn-dance, it's all go!"

"I could *ask* her ..."

Aveyard pointed to the telephone, politely went into the kitchen while Bruton made his call. He came back when he heard Jim shout his name. He was holding on to the telephone receiver. "My wife wants to know what she should wear ..." he asked.

Aveyard shrugged his shoulders. "Why ask me?" he said helplessly. Jim held the receiver close to his mouth. "The Super-intendent agrees with me," he said, "you should wear your skirt and blouse. You know, the one I like, the blue one ..." He made arrangements to pick her up, and then put down the telephone. "She wanted to wear a trouser suit!" he said.

"I bet she'd have looked very nice in it!" Aveyard said gallantly. Sergeant Bruton's wife was a good looking, homely woman, who, he imagined, could wear anything successfully.

"What are we looking for tonight?" Bruton asked. "I don't suppose we're going just for the pleasure of an evening out ...?"

"Cheeky monkey! and here am I spending ten new pence each for three tickets! Imagine what the Chief'd say if we put three tickets for a dance on my expense account ...! Anyway I suppose as much as anything we're looking for the reason Stanley Robinson murdered his wife ... if he did murder her! Mrs Larrapin implied that young Helen was a bit flighty. I'd like to interview Brian Sharp. I'd like to know what sort of a lad he was. London haven't come through with any information about him?"

"Hardly. It'd be like looking for the proverbial needle. We've sent 'em a description, of course, but we've no idea where he is, or even, come to think of it, if he is in London itself. He might be in one of the suburbs."

"I'd like to know."

"What about the missing boy? Do you think there's anything in that?" Consider all the possibilities, keep an open mind, it's the only way with police work. Nothing ever is as it seems; the criminal mind follows devious paths.

Aveyard thought a while then shook his head. "No, I don't think there's a connection. He's had a scare. Pinching lead off a roof, the old lady, what's her name ..."

"Olive Abbott."

"... she calls it sacrilege, and the kid does a bunk. No, I just can't see a connection. It isn't as if he was one of the lads who carried the Guy. I could understand it if one of the Bragg kids had gone missing." Aveyard got up and poured a drink for each of them from the quart beer bottle on the sideboard. "We'll have to get some supper somewhere," he said.

"Well, since you're being so generous and paying for the barn-dance, I'll treat you and my wife to supper. There's a

113

restaurant on the road to Ulton, that pub the Flying Fox …"

"So that's settled. Barn-dance, supper, and an early night!"

"I'll agree to that!" Bruton said.

## CHAPTER TWENTY-ONE

Bobby Smailes used to play football for Birton until a kick dislocated his knee-cap and put him out of the game for ever. He was just the type of man the brewery was looking for; the directors of the Birton Football Club gave him a golden handshake, and with his insurance money, he was able to take the Flying Fox on the Birton Road, midway between Ulton and Birton. The pub had been allowed to go to seed; he set to and cleaned the place throughout, had the brewery install new bar equipment, closed the old and decrepit skittles room, knocked down a wall between it and the barn outside, and opened a restaurant. He took on as chef an Italian who had been working as a waiter in a restaurant in Northampton; the Italian was married to an English woman and had a son and two daughters, all of whom found employment at the Flying Fox.

Bobby Smailes spent more of his time in front of the bar than behind it. Antonio Giovanni managed the catering, Mrs Giovanni had been a bar-maid before she married, and as far as the accountant from Wellingborough could tell, both were scrupulously honest.

Bobby was in the bar when Aveyard, Sergeant and Mrs Bruton arrived. "Hey up," he said, "lock the till. We've got the law in!" Bruton, a football fan, waved cheerfully to him, and Smailes came across to them. "That's a nasty business in Ulton," he said, "you working on it?"

Bruton introduced Superintendent Aveyard and Mrs Bruton. Saturday night the Flying Fox was jammed to the doors, but since they were early he found a table for them. "Another half an hour," he said, "and they'll be queueing even to get into the Gents!" He insisted on buying a drink for them at the bar, then as soon as their table was ready, he escorted them through into the high raftered barn restaurant. Aveyard had never been

115

there before. "You've done a good job with this conversion!" he said, "it must have cost a packet!"

"I don't do anything by halves ..." He'd had a reputation as a thrusting player, a fearless tackler, who pushed Birton up the league table. Aveyard guessed he'd brought the same ambitions to the restaurant business. "Now what are you going to have?" he said, handing each of them a menu. There were two sections; one a printed list of the standard dishes, fillet, rump, and minute steak, plaice grilled on the bone, halibut with prawn sauce, pheasant, rabbit pie, boeuf bourguignonne, veal Holstein; the other was a typewritten list of the day's specialities, steak and kidney pie, braised beef, veal escalop, spaghetti neapolitain, gnocchi, with ensalada mixta. "Cater for all tastes here," Bobby said proudly: "and there's a wine list on the back." He left them in peace at the table with a cheerful, "Give us a shout if they don't treat you right!"

"I do wish you'd let me wear my trouser suit," Mrs Bruton said, glancing around at some of the high fashions at the adjacent tables. "You look very nice," he assured her, looking at Aveyard for confirmation.

"You're a sight for tired eyes," Aveyard said.

Reassured, she studied the menu. "Order anything you want," Sergeant Bruton said, "it's not often I get the chance to give you a treat!" He knew her so well; if he didn't prompt her she'd select the cheapest dishes on the menu as a matter of course, a woman careful and thrifty in all she did. Aveyard was right, she was a sight for eyes sore from looking at these overdressed over made-up dolly birds. He touched her hand with pride. Wouldn't think, to look at her, she'd made that blouse herself, and the skirt. A touch of make-up, hair nicely brushed back, not showy, not gaudy, just, well, nice! "Go on," he said, "order something special!"

"All right," she said, "since you insist, I'll have something I've never in my life tasted ... I'll have the pheasant!"

"Pheasant for one, with game chips and all the trimmings, steak and kidney pie for two, and a bottle of Macon." Nothing to start with, because they were in a bit of a hurry. The young waiter's face was expressive with disappointment. So sorry, no pheasant that night. Simply no pheasant. When Mrs Bruton settled for halibut with prawn sauce they changed the wine to Chablis.

Bobby Smailes came back to their table when they were drinking coffee, and insisted they accept a brandy each on the house. "Got to keep in with the cops, haven't I?" he said and though he was joking there was an underlying note of seriousness in his voice, which Aveyard resented. Why couldn't people treat the police as ordinary human beings? Aveyard had intended to buy a brandy for Sergeant and Mrs Bruton, a personal gesture. But Bobby Smailes insisted. "Was the meal all right?" he asked, when the waiter went to fetch the brandy.

"Very good," Mrs Bruton said, "though I was disappointed not to have the pheasant. It's something I've always meant to try ..."

"Come tomorrow," Bobby said, "lunch on the house, and I personally will guarantee pheasant!"

"You'd better be careful, I might just take you up on that," Mrs Bruton said, laughing. She wasn't the sort to cadge a free lunch from anybody. Outside the Flying Fox, they sat in Aveyard's car. "It's my night for trying new things," Mrs Bruton said, "I've never been to a village barn-dance, either!" Sergeant Bruton touched her wrist and beckoned for her to be quiet. He'd seen the look on Aveyard's face as Aveyard sat there, the engine of the car not running. Bruton was used to that 'look'. The Superintendent was 'thinking'. Mrs Bruton, a policeman's wife, understood.

"No pheasant on the menu tonight," Aveyard said, musing. "And yet pheasant is on the printed menu, not the typed page, and that means pheasant delivered regularly. Fast in, fast out, with a quick turnover. But with that number of tables, he'd need a quantity ..."

"And Blatsoe's looking for somebody stealing his pheasants regularly, in quantity!"

"Bobby Smailes guarantees there'll be pheasant by lunch-time tomorrow. He's got none tonight. You saw the way he was all over us, free drinks at the bar, brandy on the house; if he'd had so much as a scrap of pheasant, he'd have given it to us ..."

"Robbery, poaching, not our detail!" Sergeant Bruton reminded him.

117

Aveyard turned to look at him. How do you explain a hunch to a man who knows procedures backwards and forwards, and sticks to the book because it's right to do so. "Nobody would have dared out last night to nick pheasant in Ulton, considering the number of policemen looking for young Bert."

"That could account for pheasant not being on Bobby Smailes menu, but it still doesn't alter the fact that poaching isn't our detail; you know how keen the Chief is that we stick to our assignments. We could ring the duty officer ..."

"On a hunch? Reasonable suspicion? They'd laugh at us!"

"Do you mind if I make a suggestion?" Mrs Bruton said. The Sergeant looked at her, vaguely disapproving.

"I know I shouldn't interfere," she said, "but why don't we all go to the barn-dance as planned, and then I'll drive Jim's car home on my own while you two go for a midnight stroll. Both of you look as if a walk'll do you good, and don't forget Bobby Smailes promises pheasant by lunch-time tomorrow!"

"One thing is certain," Aveyard said, "Bobby Smailes isn't pinching 'em! He wouldn't be so cocky about 'em if he was ..."

## CHAPTER TWENTY-TWO

The old village had turned out in strength for the barn-dance, and only Herbert Larrapin, Roger Blatsoe, Amy Dunkley and Bill Hopton were absent. Even Benny Latham turned up, with his wife Stephany, and their four daughters. Esther Larrapin stood behind an improvised bar across the corner of the Church Hall on which earlier her husband had racked a barrel of beer. Jo Elks behind a similar table across the other corner, dispensed ham sandwiches, parkin, and of course sausage rolls. The admission ticket, price ten new pence, had two detachable corners and was printed with a number. The detachable corners gave the bearer a plate of free food, and a free drink, beer for the grown ups, tizer, lemonade and dandelion and burdock for the young ones. First helping free, second helping had to be paid for. During the evening there'd be a draw out of a hat, with prizes for the lucky numbers. The band had come from Birton, a lady pianist, fiddler, saxophone, man with a concertina, and an accordionist. The fiddler, well known in the county, also did service as a caller. Most of the dances were Western in origin, with a generous sprinkling of waltzes, veletas, and even a few Scottish numbers such as the Dashing White Sergeant which in the hands of these strongly rhythmic players came out like a cowboy's romp. A pop group known as The Everlasting had been booked to play during the interval; the previous year the innovation had proved a great success with the youngsters, many of whom had requested The Everlasting play the main part of the evening, and the Birton Western and Folk Dance Ensemble be relegated to the interval. But how can you do that, the vicar asked, to a group of people who've 'obliged' you for fifteen years without fail, and for a fee so modest it could hardly cover expenses?

Superintendent Aveyard, and Sergeant and Mrs Bruton, were

119

the only strangers there, though the villagers greeted them with a show of cordiality. Sylvia Bragg led Mrs Bruton to the small room set aside as a ladies' cloakroom; Aveyard and the Sergeant put their top coats in a small room beside the stage.

"Your husband not here, Mrs Larrapin?" Aveyard asked, as he waited for his free pint of beer.

"Somebody has to stay in the pub; it's against the law to close down during licensing hours ... but of course you know that," she said, laughing. "Anyway, he'll be along after he's closed for the night—we shall be doing the last waltz together ..."

The caller was in full song, and Sergeant and Mrs Bruton stepped out onto the dance floor to obey him. "Partner to the left, Partner to the right, doe see doe, and do it just right, gentlemen forward gentlemen back, doe see doe down the railroad track!" He tucked the violin beneath his chin and the wild strains bounced round the hall, riding the melody of the accordion and the saxophone.

About thirty people were dancing with varying degrees of confidence. Aubrey Bollard had encouraged Iris Latham and in the words of her mother 'they made a fine couple'. Aubrey she thought, is a nice boy, and he'll have a good business to come into when his Da's gone. She beamed approvingly. Benny Latham was standing by the beer table. He'd had his free pint, and had bought another; when he saw Aveyard standing on his own he beckoned to him. "Come on," he said, "have a pint!" Aveyard looked at his flushed face. Benny had obviously spent some time in The Bell, getting up courage to come here. "Yes, thanks, I'll have a pint," Aveyard said. They stood together, watching the dancing. "Does it right well," Benny said, looking at the Sergeant. He danced precisely, clearly dependent on the rhythm of the music, Mrs Bruton light in his arms, looking as though with a better partner, she could really go to town. "He does everything well, my Sergeant," Aveyard said, "as a lot of people have found to their cost. Though, come to think of it, he slips up sometimes ..."

Benny Latham grunted, finished his beer. Aveyard beckoned to Esther Larrapin, who filled Benny's glass and put it down beside him. Benny picked it up, drank a quarter of it in one gulp. Aveyard had not expected him to say thank you.

"Yes, he searched in the ashes of that bonfire, my Sergeant did," Aveyard said, watching the dancing, "but never a trace did he find of a piece of chain. Now isn't that strange? There should have been a piece of chain there, because you yourself used one to fasten the Guy to the pole ..."

"Back on that old business, are we?" Benny said.

"Doesn't it seem strange to you, that there should be no chain there?" Aveyard asked. "Particularly when you remember so clearly you used a piece ... Somebody might think you were having us on, since there was no chain there ..." Repetition does it sometimes. Over and over again until the person you're talking to becomes sick and tired of hearing the same words. Benny was the kind to break that way; a more intelligent person can shut his mind to it. Not a lout like Benny. "I mean, it isn't as if *chain* would melt, is it, Benny? I mean, that piece of *chain* you used to tie the Guy to the post. *Chain* doesn't melt, does it, in a fire as weak as that one ...?"

"Don't keep on about it," Benny said. "Maybe I was wrong. How can I remember? It was over a fortnight ago. Maybe I used a chain, maybe a bit of string or rope, who knows, all that time ago ..."

"You *should* remember, Benny. After all, it was you told me you'd used a bit of chain, to tie the Guy to the post."

"Don't keep going on about it," Benny said loud, as he slammed his beer pot empty onto the table. Several people looked at him but no-one chose to interfere. Benny was known to be a bad lot when in beer, with his temper roused. Aveyard beckoned to Mrs Larrapin again, and again she filled the pot. "You trying to get me drunk?" Benny asked though not too truculent to accept the free drink.

"Now why should I do that, all because of a piece of chain?"

Benny drank greedily from the pot, then placed the pot on the table. "All right, Mr Bloody Clever," he said, "if you must know, it wasn't a piece of chain I used!" Aveyard almost sighed with relief, as bored with his own repetition as Benny had been.

"What was it, Benny?"

"You'll never believe me. It was, a piece of barbed wire ..."

121

They'd found a piece of barbed wire, burned in the ashes of the fire. Come to think of it, Aveyard had looked twice at it; the barbed wire had been twisted into an odd shape.

"Where did you get the barbed wire from, Benny?" Aveyard asked, his voice quiet.

"That's why I said you wouldn't believe me. It was twisted round the Guy's forehead, in a ring, twisted into a ring like it was a crown or something ..."

"And you untwisted one, maybe two rings of it, and used that to lash the body to the pole, leaving the rest of the ring hanging behind. And you didn't make too good a job of it and the barbed wire was only holding by one small bent bit, maybe because you caught your finger on the barbs, eh Benny, and then when the heat got to it the barbed wire expanded a bit, sprung itself, and the Guy came tumbling down ... is that right, Benny, is that right?"

"Bloody know-all, aren't you?" Benny said as he drained the pot of beer and walked across the dance floor to the gents, pushing his way through the dancing couples and the doe see does.

Olive Abbott was sitting in a high chair along one side of the Hall. "I allus come," she said to Aveyard. "It's my privilege, as the oldest surviving person in the village, to draw the raffle and present the prizes. Then I'll go home ..."

"Can I sit with you a minute?" Aveyard asked.

"Mek room for the policeman," Olive said to Sally Latham sitting beside her. "Here, tek my ticket, and go and get yourself a lemonade and a bit of summat to eat." She watched the six years old girl scamper up the side of the room. "Half starved, all the Latham kids have been," she said as Aveyard sat in the chair beside her.

"Crown of thorns," Aveyard said, looking closely at her face.

"For Jesus, our Lord," she said.

"For the Guy ..."

"That's right," she said.

"A very good touch. Did you think of it?"

"Yes, all my own work as you might say ..."

"But our Lord was crucified, dead and buried ..."

"Dust to dust, ashes to ashes ..."

"There was a dead body in that Guy ..." Watch her wrinkled

122

old face, watch her eyes for tears. But tears there are none, and the wrinkles hide every expression of inner feeling. She turned her face towards him. "You're a young man," she said, "but you'll learn. Some stones are better left without turning!"

"Tell me about the Guy," he persisted.

"I made it, as I allus do. Sewed it, as allus. This year I wound a bit o' barbed wire round its brow. Seemed fitting, somehow, seemed fitting. The Bragg lads fetched it."

"Where was it, I mean, where did they fetch it from?"

"Where I made it, on the floor in the hall."

He sat by her side when the music ended and the caller announced there would now be a Prize Draw, and following that The Everlasting would play for their Delight and Delectation. Everyone present put his ticket on the stage, and the Reverend Francis Elks, above suspicion, shuffled them into a large trilby hat. Then the trilby hat was carried triumphantly over to Olive Abbott, who made a great display of closing her eyes before she placed her hand inside the hat to draw the first prize. "Number seventeen," the vicar called out, "Number seventeen."

"That was mine," Sophie Blatsoe called. Francis Elks turned the ticket over and sure enough Miss S. Blatsoe had been printed on the back.

When the tickets had been drawn, and the prizes distributed, Olive Abbott got up, ready to leave.

"I'll take Mrs Abbott home," said Aveyard.

Together they walked slowly through the darkened village, around the small green on which the Bonfire had been laid. There was a light in the Dunkley house, though Fred Dunkley had been at the barn-dance, acting as doorman.

"That'll be Amy sitting up," Olive said.

"Are you all right to put yourself to bed?" Aveyard asked, "or shall I knock on Amy's door?"

"I've been putting myself to bed for a long time, young lad," Olive said. They turned into Tingdene Way. The wind whistled down at them from the northwest, a cold biting blow. "That's a sorrowful wind when you haven't much flesh left on your old bones," she said, as they turned into her cottage. The door was not locked. Aveyard followed her past the glass showcase that

123

contained her wedding dress. Inside the cottage was clean and shining. A fire had been left burning in the grate, damped down with a thin coating of slack. She pushed the poker into the slack and twisted it; the flames shot through almost immediately. A blackened kettle stood on the metal fireside; she moved it across until it caught the heat of the fire and at once it started to sing quietly.

"Cup of tea?" she asked.

"Yes, please, if it's not keeping you up ..."

"I shan't be going to bed for a while," she said.

The cottage had only one room downstairs divided by a centre staircase. On one side of the staircase was her 'day room', containing a sewing machine on an iron frame with a foot treadle, with a large flat table top next to it. On a shelf against the wall were several bolts of material, dark brown and navy blue, doubtless used once upon a time as linings for coats. In the nearside of the room was a settee, and an easy chair, covered in heavy flowered cretonne. By the fire was a stiff backed wooden chair, the arm of which showed the dull patina of long use. Beneath the window which overlooked the street was a table covered by a white table cloth. On it a knife and fork, a spoon, and a cup upturned on its saucer. There were heavy curtains at the window, on a heavy brass rail, with a brass rod hanging down with which one could pull the curtains across. "Shall I draw the curtains for you?" Aveyard asked.

"That'd be a mercy."

The staircase ended about eight feet from the front door, which area formed itself into a sort of entrance hall, with a stand for keeping umbrellas or walking sticks. She caught him looking at the space.

"Yes, that's where I make the Guy," she said, "right there. Meks it easier to get out of the door.

He looked up the staircase. "Interested in old cottages are you?" she said, seeing him look upwards, "go on, up the steps, have a look if you've an interest." He walked up the flight of stairs, which had been covered with a thin carpet wearing at the edge of the stair-treads, held in position by brass stair-rods. At the top of the stairs were two doors, one left, one right. He opened the one on the right. Inside was a tiny bedroom, spotlessly clean, with the bed already made and covered with a green shot silk bed-spread. Cupboard built into the wall of old oak, blackened by age. Wash stand with a mirror over it; his reflection leered back at him distorted like a funfair glass. A bowl and a water jug stood on the stand. The floorboards in this room were cut in random thicknesses, and pinned down with hand-made nails whose heads protruded. The other room was identical, except that the wall cupboard contained Olive's clothing, and there was a chest of drawers beneath the window, a wash basin with piped water and a bed-spread sewed in woollen squares. Not a single vase, not a chair, nothing in the house was out of place.

Above his head was a small door set into the wall. It had no handle. He pressed on it. It didn't move. A short flight of stairs led to the door. She was standing at the foot of the main stairs, looking up at him. "Last time that door was opened," she said, "was when they laid the piped water on. I believe there's a cistern up there, but I've never bothered to look."

"You're a very tidy woman," he said, when he was sitting by the fireplace drinking his tea, "I didn't see a spot of dust anywhere."

"At my age," she said, "it's all you've got to do with your time ... A habit I suppose. Couldn't have dust about when you were sewing somebody's wedding dress, could you, or making a shirt? It gets to be a habit, to be clean."

"You're a very remarkable woman," he said.

# CHAPTER TWENTY-THREE

Aveyard buttoned his overcoat as he came out of Olive Abbott's cottage. The barn-dance had finished, and he passed several people on their way home, laughing and calling to each other in a festival spirit that owed little to alcohol, and much to the relief of the tensions of the previous night. Amy Dunkley, standing in the door of her cottage, saw the Superintendent and came quickly down the path to the front gate. "Not found him, have you?" she asked, though her voice was without hope.

"No," he said, "but he'll turn up and we're still looking." It was his personal conviction the boy was hiding, as his father said, somewhere in a barn. Stan Coulson 'thought' he'd lost a pair of trousers, Bill Hopton was missing a jersey, Tom Bollard suspected an old donkey jacket and a pair of boots had disappeared, though he couldn't be certain. The case had been passed to Division; they had a system for dealing with Missing Persons and the matter was now out of Aveyard's hands; though he sympathised with the Dunkley parents, he had to concentrate his efforts on the problem of two 'suspicious deaths', each one of which bore all the marks of a murder.

Sergeant Bruton was waiting for him, as arranged, by the side of the Church. "I've got two men by Benny Latham's cottage," he said, "one front, one back."

"I hope they have infra-red eyes!"

"Ulton Lane's covered, all the way down, round the east end of the green by the wall, then all the way along to the Birton Road. Not even a cat can cross that lane without being seen!"

"You've warned 'em about Home Farm and Blatsoe's?" Those were the only two places on the east side of Ulton Lane; the Coulsons and Blatsoes the only ones with legitimate reason to

126

cross the Lane that night.

"Yes. Blatsoe's back, by the way. He's been out this evening but he got back about ten minutes ago."

"Where's he been?"

"He didn't say, but I smelled whisky!"

"On a gamekeeper's pay? Where is he now?"

"Watching the gate from inside!"

"Arthur Newsome?"

"In bed, asleep, I imagine."

"Warrant?"

"Division fixed that, and they loaned me this!" The Sergeant produced a portable radio from his overcoat pocket, drew out the whip aerial, and handed it to the Superintendent. "Number north to south down Ulton Lane," he said, "and the two outside Benny's are A and B. You're 'S'."

Superintendent Aveyard pressed the transmission key three times fast without speaking. Anyone listening to the radio would hear the carrier wave and the morse signal for 'S'. He removed his finger from the transmission button. One by one each constable carrying a radio pressed his transmission button in the morse code. Short then long for A and the front of Benny Latham's house, long and two shorts for B for the back, then each of the numerals in turn, up to eight.

They followed Benny Latham's progress in a morse code sequence; B saw him first, then A as he circled round his house. Three picked him up again outside the Bell, where Tunnet Lane joins Ulton Lane. Four brought him round the green. Five took him down the side of the wall of the Hall, round the dog leg, into the south end of Ulton Lane, by Eastfields. Six took him past Eastfields. Benny Latham must have spotted Seven sitting in a parked car at the entrance to Eastfields; he turned round and went back up the lane, Six watching him all the way. Five picked him up again, watched as Benny Latham seemed to melt into the shadow by the newly repaired gate. The moon was strong for November, and the shadows deep and intense by comparison with the lighted areas. With little cloud, the night air had already set cold. It was Six, who'd taken a position by Tom Bollard's where Church Street meets Ulton Lane on the south side of the green, who caught the flash of the moon on the shotgun barrel. His rapid pressures on the transmission key informed everyone. Aveyard looked at Bruton. Suspect armed. That signal added new dimensions to any surveillance. Especially when the weapon happened to be a shotgun, and the man who carried it skilled in its use.

Aveyard waited, his irritation visible.

"What the hell's he playing at ..." he said to Bruton, "we know it has to be a shotgun." Procedure laid down that when the weapon was identified as a shotgun, the rapid flutter of signals was followed by One or Two to indicate the number of barrels. It makes a hell of a difference to a constable, diving unarmed for the feet of a suspect, to know there's another barrel load still to come.

"That was a two-barrelled job Benny was carrying the other night," Bruton said.

Aveyard pressed the key to identify himself, then twice to warn them all of the kind of weapon the suspect was carrying.

Benny Latham ran his hands swiftly round the fastening of the gate. Just as he thought, bolted by Aubrey Bollard, but not locked. There'd be nowhere they could get a lock with keys on a Saturday afternoon. He'd counted on that when he'd forced the old lock. He spat into the palm of his hand then slowly wiped the bolt with it. The bolt slid silently back. He hadn't needed the spit, since Aubrey had oiled the bolt, but you never know, and Benny wasn't a man to take that kind of risk. He felt the two eye-bolt hinges. Good, they'd been oiled, too. Good young lad, Aubrey. Slowly he opened the gate, ducked through the opening, closed the gate behind him. He didn't bolt it.

The moon shone strongly beyond the wall. Stable block, as once was, to the left. Far away on the right, Home Farm, and Stan Coulson's three collies that couldn't be quietened. Fireman's Spinney ahead across the pasture; Blatsoe's tucked behind him on the right, hidden by the angle of the wall. A ditch runs from where he now stands, all the way to Fireman's. Down into the ditch. A thin run of water in the bottom, but nothing to worry him in his leather boots with a waterproof tongue. He'd had the boots from old Newsome; three springs ago the Cleaning Company had taken Benny on to give 'em a hand shifting furniture. It was the first and last time Benny had been in the Hall, but he'd made the work pay. Benny never did something for nothing. Well, hardly ever!

"How are you feeling?" Aveyard asked Bruton when they were standing outside the metal gate.

"Same as usual!" Bruton whispered, "wishing I was a shop assistant safe home in bed, wrapped snug for the night wi' my missis beside me ..." They opened the gate and went through. Aveyard tapped Bruton's arm. "Down quick," he hissed. He'd seen the figure in the trees just ahead, the outline of Benny Latham. But then he heaved a sigh of relief when the figure stepped out of the patch of shadow, and he saw it was Blatsoe, not Latham. Blatsoe came towards them.

"I thought he was Benny Latham," Aveyard said as he approached.

"So did I for the minute!"

Blatsoe stopped near them. "No good as poachers, you two," he said. "I could hear you thrashing about a mile off!"

"You'll have to give us lessons!"

"That bugger Benny Latham doesn't need lessons! You think he'll come back this way?"

"He left the gate unbolted, didn't he?"

"For what that's worth!"

Stan Coulson's collies started yowping, over to the right, the sound thin and bitter on the cold night air.

"Farmers' dogs!" Blatsoe said contemptuously.

They settled in the shadow of the wall, to wait. Blatsoe had wanted them to stalk Benny Latham, catch him in the act of lifting a pheasant, but Aveyard knew his men were not sufficiently skilled to get near Latham without giving themselves away. They waited an hour before they saw Benny Latham's figure rise ghostlike from the end of the ditch. He was carrying the double-barrelled shotgun cradled under his right arm. One pocket of his raincoat seemed to be bulging, but there were no traces of a dozen pheasants. Aveyard put his hand on Bruton's arm. Let Benny get to the gate. Benny walked slowly forwards, a solid figure in the softening moonlight. 'You could easily mistake him for Blatsoe,' Aveyard thought. Benny's shoulders hunched forward in the slouch that would carry him effortlessly across miles of country; he was wearing a flat-felted

129

cap similar to the one Blatsoe himself wore, though Benny's, too big, came down to his ears.

Aveyard was worried. Bruton too was worried; Aveyard could feel that without any words passing between them.

Benny arrived at the gate and pulled on it.

There was a muffled curse as he realised the gate wouldn't open. His hands and eyes, busy on the surface of the gate, quickly found and identified the wire Sergeant Bruton had twisted to keep the gate fastened. Aveyard, Blatsoe, and Bruton stepped out of the shadow of the wall. Bruton switched on his powerful torch, pointing the beam at Benny Latham. Benny whirled around, his back to the gate, the torchlight dazzling him.

"Drop the shotgun," Bruton said. This was the critical moment. At this range, he couldn't miss. Benny started to heft the gun.

"Drop it," Aveyard said, as he switched on his torch, fifteen feet away from Sergeant Bruton. Which does he aim at?

"Drop it," the Constable said from the other side of the gate, reaching through the metal foliage, his hand a pincer grip on Latham's arm. Eyes backwards and forwards, side to side.

"Don't be a fool, Benny," Blatsoe growled, "there's fifty policemen so put down the gun and don't play the fool!"

The familiar voice worked the trick. Benny bent and placed the gun carefully on the ground at his right side. Aveyard walked into the light of Bruton's torch.

"Untwist that wire," he called to the Constable outside the gate, "and tell the Inspector to call them in. Where've you been, Benny," he said.

"For a walk!"

"Where?"

"Fireman's Spinney ..."

"There isn't a pheasant within a hundred yards of Fireman's!" Blatsoe growled. "More likely he's been down to Five Acre Copse. We were going to beat that copse tomorrow!"

"What have you got in your pocket, Benny?" Aveyard asked, moving close enough to touch Benny's raincoat where it bulged.

"Why don't you find out ...?"

"Look, Benny, we can do this two ways, as you very well know. We've caught you, it's a fair catch. We've already got you on a book full of charges, trespassing, night loitering, armed with intent, possession of a firearm! Why, with a face as dirty as yours I could book you right now with wandering by night with your face *blackened* with intent and I'll bet you've never even *heard* of that one!"

Benny reached into his raincoat pocket and from it produced a plastic shopping bag. Printed on the outside of the bag was the name of a butcher in Birton. He opened the bag slowly. Inside it was a newspaper wrapped parcel and a small paper slip. He handed the slip to the Superintendent, then unwrapped an unskinned rabbit.

"I reckon that paper'll do as a receipt," he said, unsmiling. On the small piece of paper was printed a number, a price, and the blue ink words 'Received with thanks. Call again'.

"Let's have a look at that shotgun," Sergeant Bruton said. He bent down and picked it up. A hood had been screwed across the top of the hammers. The gun couldn't be broken, couldn't be loaded or fired. "Firearms Act of '68," Sergeant Bruton said bitterly, "excludes guns with covers!" Benny Latham grinned at them.

"I was taking a walk," he said, "couldn't sleep. I don't like walking without summat in my hands. Look at any country man, he'll allus have summat in his hands when he goes for a walk, isn't that right Mr Blatsoe?" Blatsoe grunted. "As for me being here, trespassing, well, I'm sorry about that, and if you ask me to leave, I'll leave. You won't catch me causing no breach of the peace by refusing to leave somebody's property when asked to do so, that you won't!"

Aveyard and the Sergeant exchanged disgusted glances. Benny Latham was right, of course. Trespassing isn't an offence, unless it can be proved the trespasser has committed or intends to commit another offence. All you can do is ask the trespasser to leave. You can't even use violence to eject him!

"Barrack-room lawyer, eh, Benny?" the Superintendent said, "well perhaps you'd be good enough to accompany my Sergeant as far as the Village School and help us with our enquiries?"

Benny Latham grinned. "I can't sleep anyway, and knowing your lads, there'll be cups of tea handed round ..." He and the Sergeant went through the gateway towards the Village School. The surveillance had been co-ordinated by Inspector Coates. "It'll be a long night for you, I'm afraid," Aveyard said to him.

"A change from sitting at that ruddy desk. What are we looking for?"

"A dozen brace of pheasants. Hidden somewhere between here and – what did you say that copse was called, Mr Blatsoe?"

"Five Acre Copse. But it's my guess he'll have hidden them in Fireman's Spinney. You can get to the Spinney easy from the back."

"Then why didn't he go that way tonight?"

"That's where I usually wait for 'im, and damn well he knows it. If it's him who's taking the pheasants," he added.

"Can you go with my lads? Give 'em a bit of guidance?"

"Be glad to, if it means nailing yon sod!" Blatsoe said.

Benny Latham had obtained a carton of tea for himself when Aveyard arrived. Bruton was sitting with him, in a small classroom off the main room. Three night men on duty in the Incidents Room, and one girl typist, tapping the keys of her machine as if a ghost was chasing her.

"Good girl," Aveyard said. Typists were not usually asked to work all night, especially on a Saturday.

She smiled back at him. "It's not often we have so many 'eye-witness' statements," she said.

"It's not often we have a pretty girl to look at this time of night," he countered. She blushed.

The Incidents Book was on Inspector Coates' table. Aveyard opened it and looked down the various notations. The Incidents Book was the Bible of any murder investigation; every action was telephoned to the man who looked after the book, every request, every suggestion. Inspector Coates made it his personal job to see that action was carried out. A good Incidents Book, and a conscientious man to keep it, could cut the work of an enquiry by half. He noted that at 11.52 a telephone call had gone to London, the most recent of a series of telephone calls attempting to trace the missing man, Brian Sharp. He noted also that a weight, height and age composite picture of Brian Sharp had been obtained by enquiries among the villagers, and the pathologist's comments had been recorded, stating that the corpse was too old. Right, he could cross that idea off in his mind, Brian Sharp was not the man on the Bonfire. Helen Robinson, he noted, had died without regaining consciousness, without speaking. Damn! If only she could have answered one question they might have discovered who had injected arsenic into her. The woman Police Inspector who had sat by her bed had left her home telephone number, in case the Superintendent wanted to question her. He made a note for her to be telephoned in the morning, and thanked.

There was no further news on the search for Bert Dunkley, according to the situation report timed for one thirty.

The Detective Chief Superintendent would be grateful for an early call from the Superintendent, as he had a meeting with the Chief Constable at ten. Aveyard signed his initials in the appropriate column, to indicate he had read the report up to that point.

"Right, Mr Latham," he said, seating himself behind the teacher's desk in the classroom, "what the devil's going on!" Dammit, even the teacher's desk was too small ...

"I don't know what you mean, Sergeant," Benny Latham said, though he was looking at Aveyard.

"I'm a Superintendent, and well you know it ..."

"Sorry, Super ..."

Aveyard came from the teacher's chair, walked slowly across the classroom and placed his face six inches from Latham's. "To call me Super," he said, "you have to wash yourself at least once a year. Yes, and clean your teeth!"

Benny Latham gulped.

"The police have great powers for the arrest and prosecution of persons who, by their actions, appear likely to commit a crime. That's word by word almost a quote from the book, *Benny!* And here's another quote for you. A *suspected person*, and that's you, *Benny*, a suspected person is a person who has acquired the character of a suspect by reason of his previous

133

conduct. Now, don't try your barrack-room lawyer stuff with me!"

A lot of people misunderstood Aveyard's mild manner; few ever did it twice. He walked back to the teacher's desk and sat down. Bruton went from the room; when he returned he was carrying three cartons of tea. He gave one to the Superintendent, put one on his own desk, and the third just out of reach of Benny Latham's hand.

"You got any cigarettes?" he asked.

Benny Latham took a packet from his pocket. Bruton placed it near the tea. "We want you to look after your lungs," he said, as Benny Latham's eyes flicked nervously from one to the other. Bruton sipped his tea; Aveyard sipped his.

"Interesting report, that one in the paper," Sergeant Bruton said. "Amnesty International. Interrogation of prisoners. Torture, all that stuff. It seems that physical torture is dying out now. No need for it. It's all psychological, these days. Keep a man on edge. Deprive him of his natural sleep. Apparently, it never fails."

"I've always said knocking a man about was a bit old-fashioned. Take Mr Latham here. Real tough guy, he is. You could bang on him all night and you'd never get a word out of him. You could stick lighted matches under his fingernails, put electric shocks on his private parts, you'd never get a dicky bird. That right, Mr Latham?"

"Think you're clever don't you ... Superintendent?"

"Not really. If we were clever, we'd both be home in bed instead of sitting here at half past three in the morning, waiting for a lad like you to take us into his confidence. That was a set-up tonight. You went into Birton this afternoon, bought a rabbit and got a receipt for it. You screwed the cover on that gun, because you know the law doesn't operate if a shotgun is incapable of being loaded and fired. You walked down Ulton Lane, looking for policemen. You spotted one at the end of Eastfields, then turned around, hoping he'd follow you. Going for a walk, late at night! Sorry I'm trespassing, but ask me to leave and I'll go quiet! Who do you think you're kidding?"

Benny Latham said nothing, held his face straight to restrain the smile. A man has pride, hasn't he, and the coppers always think they know best. He was of no account to them, wasn't that what the Superintendent had told him, the night they'd discovered the corpse on the Bonfire. That was the night he'd made up his mind to show 'em. For years now the coppers had harassed him. Everything that had ever happened in the village, old Syd Fellowes had blamed him for. Month after month, year after year, Syd had ground him down all the time. If Benny Latham had a bad reputation, well blame the coppers for that, never leaving 'im be. How many had they used tonight? God knows! And that old sod Blatsoe. No pheasants in Fireman's. Well, Benny Latham could show him a thing or two. There were pheasants in Fireman's, if you knew where to look. Ought to make *him* the gamekeeper. Nobody'd have a pheasant off him! Or a rabbit, or a hare. Still, it had been bloody satisfying tonight, walking through the grounds of the Hall with a knackered shotgun under his arm and a rabbit in his pocket, knowing they were out looking for him, knowing they'd painted him black before ever they'd started. Stay here all night if they wanted. It wouldn't worry Benny Latham to go a night without sleep! Nor it wouldn't be the first time. How many nights had he stood in Fireman's, watching Blatsoe look for poachers. How many times he watched Blatsoe pass him by, knowing damn well Blatsoe had no idea anybody was near. No bugger'd ever get within ten feet of Benny Latham without he knew about it.

"For years," he said, "you lot have persecuted me one way and another. That van o' mine is licensed and insured! Surprised, eh? Take the other night. Bricks and glass, to make a bit of a greenhouse, and what's the first thing you think, that I've nicked 'em off a building site. I bought them bricks, and I bought that glass and them windows, and if only you'd got eyes in your head you'd have recognised 'em as coming from that demolition next door to the police headquarters in Birton, when they pulled down the old County Court. Them windows, as I made the greenhouse from, come right out of the old County Court. And what's more, I have a bit of paper from the demolition contractor to prove I paid him good money! But no, you have to go jumping to conclusions because it's Benny Latham's greenhouse, and Benny Latham can do no right! When the village shop was broken into, six, seven years ago, Benny Latham must have done it. Old Syd Fellowes searched my place top to bottom three or four times, for that! Yes, and long before that, when that lad in the village raped Amy Dunkley, all because I was out and about that evening, and Amy said she thought she recognised the man as had done her. Well, I saw somebody out and about that night, and thought I recognised him, and made the mistake of telling that old bugger, Syd Fellowes."

"Watch your tongue," Sergeant Bruton said, "Constable Fellowes is dead and we won't listen to a dirty mouth like you swearing at his memory ..."

"No, Sergeant, let Mr Latham talk ..." Aveyard said, "if he's been persecuted, as he appears to claim, I want to know about it."

"What's the use ...?"

"A lot of use, if it'll stop you taking a rise out of us. All right, I'll admit you caught us fair and square tonight. You had us on a wild goose chase if that makes you happy, and if we've been unjust to you in the past, that's the least we deserve. You claim you've been persecuted. When did it start?"

"The night of the rape I suppose. Never had no bother afore that ..."

"Tell us about the rape, anything you can remember."

"Well, there's not much. I was walking about, the way I allus do. Trouble wi' me is, I can't sleep at nights. Never could. You try living in a village where everybody gets their head down at nine o'clock, and see what kind of a reputation you'll get if they happen to peer out of the bedroom windows and see you walking about. Straight away, you're the village poacher. You're also the village thief. Every time, every thing that has gone missing in this village over the last few years, it's always been Benny Latham who's taken it; and most of it from houses I've never been inside!"

"Lot of stuff missing?"

"We've got a magpie, all right!"

"What sort of things?"

"Oh, I don't know, little things mostly you wouldn't bother about."

"Money?"

Benny Latham laughed. "They look after money all right. No, not money. Take Tom Bollard. Had a little dog cart, brought it out for an exhibition of old crafts the vicar gave in the Church Hall. Tiny little thing it was, hand-made of course, but a lovely job of carpentry. More of, what you'd call an antique curiosity. Meant to be hitched on to a little dog ..."

"And it was lost?"

"At the end of the crafts show, it was missing. I'd given the vicar a bit of a hand with things, you know, putting up the trestle tables and everything, and they all swore I'd nicked it. Old Syd had my place apart looking for it."

"Let's get back to the rape," Aveyard said. "The night of the rape. You were taking a walk, I believe you said ...?"

"Yes, down Tunnet Lane. I was walking along. Late at night it was, but not too late. Suddenly, I felt the hair prickle along my arms. I know that sounds fanciful, but that's how it was. I looked around me, couldn't see nothing of course since it was dark, but I had a feeling there was somebody crouched in the hedge. Well, like a bloody fool, I walked on a bit, then I got in the hedge, at the bottom of that ash tree at the end of the lane that leads to East Lodge Farm. I'd only been there five minutes when Old Syd comes along on his bicycle. Like a fool I stepped out into the Lane, and he saw me, stopped his bike of course, asked me what I was doing crouching in the hedge. Well, I felt that daft, I didn't say nothing about what I'd felt earlier, so I told him I'd been urinating as was every man's need. He read the riot act to me, and that put my back up and well, one thing led to another, and we had a bit of a ding-dong."

"You hit a Police Constable?" Sergeant Bruton asked.

"No, I didn't exactly hit him, but I leaned forward and he stumbled over his bike and swore I'd pushed him. Which I never meant to!"

"And then you carried on walking ...?" Aveyard persisted.

"He rode off one way, I walked the other. But as I turned round, I got a flash of a face. Now here's the funny thing. I knew as I knew that face, but I couldn't for the life of me tell you whose it was. I felt, sure as I'm sitting here, that I knew that lad, whoever he was, but I couldn't stick a name on his tail ... Well, not fifteen minutes after that, Amy Dunkley was straddled, and of course, when she said it'd been dark and she didn't get too good a look at whoever'd done her, but she *thought* she recognised him as being a local, and Old Syd knew I'd been about, straight away he jumped to the conclusion I was the one who'd done it. And nothing I could ever say or do would convince him otherwise. They had the big lads out from Birton, and the doctors an' all, and very embarrassing that was, fair shamed me they did ..."

"Yes, I know about medical inspections in cases of suspected rape ..." Aveyard said dryly.*

"But they never found nothing. Neither on me, nor on her to tie in with me. And at my own say so they stood me up in front of her, and 'Amy,' I said, 'I never laid a finger on you, you know that's true, don't you lass?' and she was bound to agree. But nobody never forgot. Guilty I was, and guilty I've stayed to this very day. Old Syd never let me forget, not for one minute!"

Aveyard stood up, walked round the room a minute or more. "You can go home to bed," he said. "I shall read the files on that rape, and Constable Fellowes' reports, and if I find you've been victimised or persecuted as you call it, you'll hear from me again. Yes, and I expect from the Chief Constable. But if I ever catch you setting me up again like you have done tonight, that'll be your lot. You've had your bit of revenge. But if ever you do it again ... You understand!"

Benny Latham nodded.

"Right, off you get!"

Benny Latham got up; Sergeant Bruton handed him his packet of cigarettes. "You want to give them up," he said. "Every one of them's a nail in your coffin. But I'm only telling you for your own good!" he added hastily, catching the Superintendent's eye.

* See *Cock-pit of Roses.*

# CHAPTER TWENTY-FOUR

## SUNDAY MORNING

Benny Latham's up, bright and early, despite the short sleep. A greenhouse full of chrysanthemums to get ready for the Christmas trade, a couple of gross of hyacinths in pots, a dozen opuntias, grown from seed. Hardly worth the bother, the opuntias, though he'll get four bob a pot from the greengrocer in Birton market who sells his stuff on the side. 'Fifty feet o'glass and an acre of land, that's all I need,' Benny Latham muses, 'then they could all go and get stuffed!'

Brian Sharp wakens in a hotel in King's Cross, pulls on his trousers, his shirt. He'll be glad to get back home, where he can breathe again, out of the airless city. Twenty minutes to catch the train. *News of the World*, cup of stewed tea off a barrow.

Sunday morning early, tea in bed on a tray with a linen cloth for Sergeant Bruton. "It's quarter to seven," Mrs Bruton says softly, tickling the side of his nose. He sits up slowly.

"You ought not to have bothered to get up," he says, "but thank you for the tea!"

"Breakfast's ready, but you've time for a wash and a shave." Sergeant Bruton hates to eat breakfast before he's scraped the razor over his face. She knows too that he prefers his bacon done to a crisp, his eggs soft, his toast dry.

"I don't think I'll be able to manage this afternoon," he says, "I'm sorry!"

"It's all right," she says, "I've already telephoned our Elsie not to expect us."

"You could go on your own!"

"No, it wouldn't be the same, not on my own."

Sunday morning early and Bert Dunkley wakens. He listens

carefully, as he's been instructed, then goes down. "Is everything all right?" she calls, from her bedroom.

"Yes, I'm just off to the bathroom!"

"Not got an upset stomach, have you?"

"No, everything's all right," he says.

"You'll go back to sleep, won't you. It's early to be getting up," she says.

Sunday morning early and Inspector Coates writes in the Incidents Book, recording the twelve brace of pheasants one of the Constables found with necks pulled in Fireman's Spinney, hidden in a canvas sack beneath a blackberry bush. Four of 'em got brambles in their hands extracting the sack, including Blatsoe the gamekeeper who should have known better. Inspector Coates ends his notation with an instruction—'check Benny Latham's hands for brambles', then signs himself off duty for a bath and a few hours of sleep.

The Incidents Room had that odour of all night smoking when the Superintendent returned shortly after half past seven on Sunday morning. Three typists had been at work since seven o'clock, and the last of the eye-witness interviews had been typed, copied, and bound into the Statements Book. Aveyard sat down to read, not with an expectation of uncovering any new facts, but to give himself a composite picture of the life of the village and the events of the Friday night. He studied the book of eight by tens the photographer had supplied; none of them revealed anything new.

The Reverend Francis Elks tolls the bell, fantasising that, once, just once, everyone in the village, and in Eastfields, will hear the call like hungry soldiers summoned to the cookhouse. 'Perhaps I ought to announce the services by blowing a bugle from the top of the belfry,' he thought, smiling at his own whimsy. Nancy Hopton rushes from the church, caught by the bell in the act of shining brasses, a tin of metal polish and a soft duster in her hand. She'll be back for evensong, but as a customer, not an unpaid member of staff!

Sergeant Bruton arrived at eight o'clock, by which time the Incidents Room was fully manned. Bruton glanced quickly through the Incidents Book. "Are we going to pull in Benny Latham?" he asked the Superintendent.

Aveyard shook his head. "I don't believe it," he said. "One pheasant, two, perhaps as many as four, but I can't see him handling a dozen brace. That's twenty-four birds. You don't just hawk round twenty-four birds ..."

"He's got a market for 'em ... The Flying Fox ...?"

"We don't know that, do we. We suspect, but don't know it."

"Shall I go over there, ask a few questions ...?"

"You're the one was saying it was none of our business. Let Division handle it. I'd like to know as discreetly as possible where they buy their pheasants. But discreetly. Somehow, I don't think it was Benny Latham, I don't think he has the ability to mastermind a deal like that. One or two pheasants now and again, that's his style, but not a regular order delivered once a week ... And if it's not him, I don't want whoever's responsible to be frightened off."

Bruton made a notation in the Incidents Book. "I'll ring Division about nine o'clock," he said, "and they can send somebody round just before lunch-time, to check if pheasant is on the menu ... No news of Brian Sharp, I notice."

"He'll come home, all in good time."

"No news of that boy, Bert Dunkley?"

"Somebody's sheltering him, you can be certain of that ..."

"I see Division's got a cough out of the lead boys; four of 'em from Eastfields." There was no reply from the Superintendent. Sergeant Bruton looked round the Incidents Room. "You've got to hand it to Inspector Coates," he said, fingering the book, "he runs a tidy ship ..." Again there was no response; Bruton could see the Superintendent had something on his mind. Let it stew a while; ten to one it'd be nothing the Sergeant could understand. Facts and figures, that's what the Sergeant liked. A well run Incidents Room, statements correctly typed and annotated ...

"Several things bothering me," Bill Aveyard said, "but for the life of me, I can't say why. Did you hear Benny Latham last night say there had been a lot of stealing in and around the village. That's unusual, isn't it? Villagers have a way of dealing with petty pilferers. Stealing like that's a town disease, people nipping into hotel rooms, or along the back doors of terrace houses. I know you'll say it's none of our business, but I can't help feeling we're going to understand these two murders better the more we know about the life in Ulton."

"Division could send a few men round; a few lads are waiting in the next room with nothing to do ..."

"Let's get out a questionnaire, send 'em round with it. You never know ..."

Together they formulated a list of questions designed to obtain information about village thefts. When they'd completed it, the Sergeant gave it to one of the girls who typed it, then copied it on the machine.

"You said there were several things ..." Bruton reminded the Superintendent.

"This is one for you. I was in Olive Abbott's house yesterday evening; ten or fifteen minutes. Without me saying anything to you in advance, I'd like you to make an excuse and see Olive Abbott. Maybe you could be the one to interrogate her about possible thefts from the house. When you get back, give me your general impressions ..."

"What am I looking for?"

"I haven't the faintest idea ..."

A Constable approached. "Call for you, Superintendent," he said. It was Doctor Samson. "I've just been talking with Mr Bage," he said, "and I think you ought to know this. That child Mrs Robinson was expecting. A comparison of the blood groups proves the child wasn't fathered by Mr Robinson. Couldn't possibly be his child."

"I didn't think it was," Aveyard said dryly, "and what's more, I imagine that child was the motive for the murder!"

"One more thing," Doctor Samson said, "Stanley Robinson's been taking arsenic regularly for the last six months. Small doses, but enough to build up a cumulative effect. If the doses had continued, he'd have been dead in another two months ..."

Aveyard had been making notes on the pad before him while Doctor Samson talked. "No evidence of the method of administration, I suppose?" he asked.

"No, but it must have been taken orally."

"And you're certain it's been going on for some time?"

"Arsenic grows with hair and by checking how far along

it is we can tell for how long the arsenic has been administered. You know, like rings in a tree trunk tell you its age. There can be no doubt about it."

"Let me put a supposition to you," Aveyard said, "Stanley Robinson takes his tea every morning in his greenhouse. There's arsenic in that greenhouse. Is it possible that by carelessness, he was giving himself a dose of arsenic every morning in his tea. Let's say he was stirring his tea with a piece of stick, or a spoon that had arsenic on it, would that account for his regular intake?"

"How, that's all you're interested in ..." he said. "You don't care so much why. How, when, what ..." Doctor Samson snapped on the other end of the line.

"I might say, Doctor Samson, that if you had informed Division you were treating a man twice accused of murder and on each occasion found not guilty, we might have been able to keep an eye on Mr Robinson, and perhaps even prevented the death of his wife ..." He heard Samson suck his breath in annoyance.

"You go too far, Superintendent," Doctor Samson said, his voice cold. "You especially should know a doctor has a duty to his patient. When Mr Robinson came south, completely cleared of charges the police had brought against him in the north, completely exonerated in court, he became my patient. Since that time, I've done my best to look after him medically. It's not up to me to give you such information as would enable you to start the persecution where the northern police left off!"

"That's the second time I've heard about police persecution in the last twelve hours," Superintendent Aveyard said, "and frankly, Doctor, I'm getting a little hot under the collar about it. I wasn't asking you to disclose the nature either of Mr Robinson's illness, or of your treatment. But associated closely with the police as you are, I'd have thought your common sense would have let you inform Division that Mr Robinson had come to live among them; they could have informed Constable Fellowes, who could have kept a general eye on the situation. Without persecution, as you call it. As it is, a situation has developed; Mrs Robinson has obviously been messing about

143

with another man, if what Mr Bage says is correct and I don't doubt that for a moment, and the consequences have been tragic."

"What do you suggest Constable Fellowes, in all his wisdom, might have done?" Doctor Samson asked, his voice still icy.

"I don't know, Doctor. Fellowes had lived in the village for twenty years or more. He was a sensible chap. I'm certain he would have found some way of acting, if he'd known Robinson's background and history."

"What's happened to your ideas of justice, Superintendent? The man had been accused twice, and twice he'd been found Not Guilty. So far as our courts are concerned, his slate was clean."

"I'm not talking about justice, Doctor. I leave that to the agitators and the mindless do-gooders! I'm talking about practicality. Obviously Robinson was disturbed. He must have been, or you wouldn't have left instructions with your wife that he was to be given your telephone number in the path lab. When is the medical profession going to wake up to the fact that an ounce of prevention, and that means forewarning, is better than all your pills, all your injections, all your placebos and palliatives ..."

"You're being unnecessarily offensive, Superintendent," Doctor Samson said, "but oddly enough, I take your point. I'm sorry. I think you're right. I should have let somebody know. The Robinson situation was very dangerous. Without going too far I can tell you he was in a very disturbed state when I took him on as a patient. I thought I'd calmed him down a bit, but it seems I was wrong, doesn't it? I never truly believed there was a danger of him killing his wife ..."

"Now hold on, Doctor. Who's talking about persecution now ...? I haven't said he killed his wife. I'm holding him in custody, yes, since he is a possible suspect, but I'm not prejudging him. It's up to us to find if there is sufficient evidence to prosecute him. And until we do that, so far as I'm concerned, he is an innocent man!"

Doctor Samson chuckled on the other end of the line. "I'm making a porridge of the Robinson affair, am I not ...?"

"Because *at the moment* it doesn't seem there's any alternative suspect, we all tend to think the one we've got is the one who's done it ... But now that my Sergeant has found the hypodermic needle fastened in the chair, it changes the whole complexion of the case. That hypodermic could have been put in that chair any time during the past week or more, especially since Mr Bage can learn nothing from the oxidation of the arsenic. Apparently you can leave that stuff out in the air for months without deterioration. And here's another thought for you, Doctor Samson. That chair in which the hypodermic was fastened was an unusual one to find in a kitchen. Robinson's an older man, much more likely to have a favourite chair than his young and no doubt sprightly wife. Whenever did you see a woman using a chair in the kitchen? I think that was Stanley Robinson's chair; in which case, who was the arsenic intended for? Stanley Robinson, or his wife? It's worth thinking about, especially since you tell me he's been receiving small regular doses over a long period of time. Was this dose supposed to be for him, a heavy dose to kill him? Has someone been poisoning him slowly, over a long period of time, and decided suddenly to knock him off quickly on account of an emergency such as a pregnancy ...?"

There was no reply from Doctor Samson. Then, finally, "Oh dear," he said, "I *have* made a porridge of this. Looking back over the Robinson case I can see that, if I'd been thinking objectively, I could have been of great help. The symptoms he explained to me were consistent with nervous disorder, an indeterminate feeling of nausea, occasional vomiting, slight abdominal pains. Of course I checked for appendix and similar malfunctions, but I never thought of arsenic poisoning. I thought it was nervous in origin ..."

"We all make mistakes, Doctor, but I do wish you'd said something to Division about it ..."

"Yes, I can see that now. Oh dear, there are so many things these days, it's so hard to know when to speak and when not ..."

"One thing that's puzzled me, Doctor, and maybe this comes in to the category of things I shouldn't ask, but why wasn't Mrs Robinson on the Pill ...?"

"Her husband wanted a family. We discussed it of course, but I had a feeling that a family would help his nervous dis-

145

orders. Give him someone to think about other than himself, if you know what I mean ..."

"Yes, I know. Poor devil. It he'd let his wife go on the Pill, who knows, all of this might never have happened ! While we're discussing village folks, and since none of this is being recorded or written down, there isn't anything else you'd like to tell me about the villagers? I repeat, in the strictest confidence of course !"

"There's nothing to tell. Not that I know of ... Arthur Newsome is dying, I don't know if that's the sort of detail you're interested in ...?"

"Poor devil; what's wrong with *him*?"

"Cancer, I'm afraid. Inoperable, malignant. He won't see the winter out. I've got him on drugs of course but about February we shall have to take him in somewhere as a terminal case."

"Anybody know?"

"His solicitor, of course, Marks of Birton. He telephoned to verify my diagnosis, ask if there was any need for a second opinion. I'd already had one of course, oddly enough from Mr Bage."

"What'll happen to the estate?"

"I don't know details, but I believe Mr Newsome is giving it to the Council for low cost housing development."

"So Blatsoe will be out of a job ...?"

"I imagine so ..."

"He's not one of your patients, is he?"

"Yes, he is, though I never have cause to see him. He's as sound as a bell ! Look, I'm dreadfully sorry about Robinson," the doctor said, hesitantly. "Do you think I ought to make a report to the Chief Constable?"

Aveyard thought for a moment. Police discipline dies hard. The Chief Constable was a man who liked to be kept informed, not only of the facts, but of the nuances of any particular case.

"I'm afraid that decision you must make for yourself," he said.

Sunday morning. and the men from Division, some of them borrowed from neighbouring Divisions, walk round the village knocking on doors. Question One : is there any object, however small, however insignificant, that you have lost during the past year? Many of the answers are not even worth writing down, of course. 'Our Sophie can't find her slippers, I've lost my best sewing scissors, Dad never knows where he's put his glasses!' In the Incidents Room, Inspector Coates, restored by a few hours sleep, takes the completed questionnaires and from them begins to discover a pattern, clear as folk-weave. Over twenty items of a specific nature had been 'missed' during the past year. One pair of tortoise shell opera glasses, one box filled with grandmother's jade 'Jewellery'. Three separate copper jelly moulds. One copper camper's kit. One leather covered writing box. One silver plate cruet set. A pair of old bottle glass decanters; the list read like the auction of the contents of an old, old, rectory. One brass bound leather covered Bible, two old portraits, one *Monarch of the Glens*, in a purple velvet covered frame studded with thousands of tiny beads. Two glass paper weights with flowers inside, lovely flowers they was, belonged to my grandma, who got 'em from hers. One whalebone corset, well, it hadn't any value, more of a curiosity really; one brass bound box containing three decanters, well, I think it's gone, but it might be in the attic somewhere, old junk really, I've been on to him for years to throw it out, and I thought he'd taken the hint at last.

Inspector Coates and Sergeant Bruton compiled a list of the articles, including the approximate date of loss. Six were within the past week. One glass case containing moths and butterflies, approximately ten inches high, four inches in diameter, on an ebony plinth. One set of brass hand-bells, six in number, mounted on an oak board inscribed 'Ulton Parish Church, 1874, Stedman Caters, five hours fifteen minutes, June 14th'. One jewellery box, approximately six inches by four inches, three inches deep, set in mother-of-pearl. One box containing brass pharmaceutical weights, and a portable scale. One Meerschaum Pipe in a leather case, and one locket, wrapped in cotton wool in a tin, said to contain a wisp of the hair of Thomas-à-Becket. The tin was given to commemorate the coronation of Queen Victoria. "It's a family heirloom is that locket," Arthur Tewson had said, "it'd grieve me no end if we didn't find it!"

"You see the pattern, Superintendent?" Bruton said.

Aveyard nodded. "They'll throw that locket away and flog

the tin!" he said, "whoever's taking it, he's looking for Victoriana, the sort of stuff that goes like hot cakes in Petticoat Lane, and the Portobello Road these days."

"It would be worth a telephone call," Jim Bruton said, "especially since the markets open on a Sunday morning!"

"Can I leave it with you?"

Bruton picked up the telephone. "I want a call to London," he said.

Olive Abbott had lost nothing. She knew where everything was in her house. "A place for everything, and everything in its place," the Sergeant murmured.

"You'll have a biscuit and a cup of coffee?"

"If you're having one yourself?"

She made him a cup of coffee in the old-fashioned way, by grinding the beans and scalding them, warming the milk in a separate pan. "I haven't tasted coffee like that," he said, "since I left my mother!"

"Happen you'd 'a done better to stay with her!"

"I've got a jewel of a wife. I'll bet your husband used to say that, too?"

She sat down, her coffee cup on a woollen mat on the three legged table beside her. "He seemed to be smitten wi' me," she said, smiling, "and I allus tried to do my best for him."

Bruton took a biscuit from the barrel she'd placed beside him, a chocolate wholemeal. "Shall you have one?" he asked politely. She shook her head. "No, I've never eaten between meal-times," she said.

She was a small, thin, gaunt faced woman, on whom the lines of life of petty duress had bitten gradually, but deeply. Her eyes were dark brown and sombre. Despite her age, or perhaps in response to her early training, he thought, she sat straight in the chair, hands folded in her lap when she wasn't drinking her coffee. The ends of her fingers were spatulate, and covered in callouses where the eye of the needle had pressed over the years. Her hands were still, avoiding unnecessary movement, but it was not the stillness of an arthritic old age. Her joints were supple even now though what little flesh she carried had become emaciated with age and the skin was taut and held the patina of old rubbed leather.

"Your Superintendent's sent you to give me the once over, hasn't he?" she asked, her eyes merry at the thought.

"He told me to come. We wanted to find out if you'd lost anything. Normal enquiry. We're asking everybody in the village."

Olive cackled, then wiped the corners of her eyes on the hem of the neat white linen pinafore she wore. "What did he tell you?" she said. "Go and see that old witch and find out what you can make of her? Your Superintendent's too sharp for the job he has. When you get to my age you realise things are never what they seem. You can't make up your mind according to what you see. It's what you feel that counts. People don't allus do as you'd expect 'em, not in this world. Build walls around people, order 'em this way and that, but inclination counts, not rules and reasons. When Amy Latham, Benny's oldest sister, Amy Coulson as now is, were married forty years ago, she would have a coloured dress. People told her, if you're not married in white there'll be tongues wagging! But she'd set her heart on a colour, and a colour she must have, and that's forty years gone. I could tell you things, I could. There's a woman in this village still sleeping in the same sheets she had when wed; she brought every one of them sheets to me, and the pillow cases. 'Olive,' she said to me, 'hearts entwined, that's what I want, hearts entwined on everything. I mean to give him a bed of love!' And that from a young gel who'd never been kissed afore her intended. Well, she's given him a bed of love, and three of the best children you'd find!"

Bruton's mind flicked like a computer through the families of the village. He couldn't help himself; it was second nature. Nancy Bollard had three children; 'Hearts entwined,' eh?

"You know who it was on the Bonfire," he said, "and you know the ins and outs of the Robinson business ...?"

"I'll not say as I *know* about the Robinson lass," she said. "They're newcomers to the village!"

"You know about Benny Latham?"

"Benny. Of course I know about 'im. Sad lad! He's a worker all right, but what chance has he had? Bill Hopton gives him summat to do from time to time, but not what you'd call a job. Benny never had the purpose in life to make the best of

149

hissen. Never had no ambition, unless it was to grow flowers, and there's no money in that to speak of. But mark my words, them as paints Benny black is storing up evil for themselves ..."

"You don't think he steals Mr Newsome's pheasants?"

"That all depends on what you mean by stealing, doesn't it? Benny's a country lad. If he walks into a field, the rabbits come looking for him. Pigeons, partridges in the old days, aye and pheasants, they used to belong to them as could catch 'em. In my day we lived off what came out of the fields. Until I was forty years of age, I never set foot in a butcher's shop. Whoever heard of folks like us buying from a butcher. It was rabbit pie on a Monday, lasting over till Tuesday, pigeons on Wednesday, game birds, hare, fish from the river, blackberry and blueberry pie from the hedgerows, and on the week-end, maybe, a joint we got from a farmer as killed his own beasts. Blood sausages, chitterlings, tripe, chicken and eggs of our own, turkeys at Christmas, ducks and geese. Benny was brought up that way. Who's to say if a pheasant crosses his path he's going to stand back and give it way so's Mr Newsome can knock it out of the sky? Benny's a country lad, and you'll never convince him taking a pheasant is stealing, anymore than you'd stop blackberries growing in the hedgerows."

"I've got the report on cactuses you wanted," Inspector Coates said, to Superintendent Aveyard. "You wouldn't believe it, but almost everybody in the village has one, right load of cactus maniacs they are. It's all these picture frame windows they've put in the new houses in Eastfields. After all, what else can you stick on a plastic side table ...?"

"How many are damaged, that's all that interests me!"

"Two!"

The Superintendent had been looking tired. Now his interest quickened.

"Two *excluding* Stanley Robinson's?"

Inspector Coates shook his head. "*Including.*"

"So there's only one! Where?"

"That artist chap, John Western!"

Aveyard whistled in surprise. "What kind?"

"It conforms to the drawing Mrs Collis gave you!"

"An opuntia?"

"Don't ask me. Anyway, it's a giant. Four feet high! Damaged down two sides. Lots of spines missing, according to the report."

"Phone Mr Bage!"

"I've already taken the liberty of doing so. He's asked for it to be brought in!"

"Well, I'll be damned. He gave us a rocket for taking in the last one!"

"He doesn't want the whole plant. Only one of the spines. Everett checked it. I reckon that boy's earned himself a commendation!"

"You'd give 'em out like cigarette coupons if I let you ... What's he done?"

"You said to be discreet about the cactuses. The story we used was that we were checking insecticides that might contain arsenic. Everett was in the Western greenhouse reading labels to make sure none contained arsenic, when suddenly he spotted this damn great cactus. But how to get a sample of the spines without letting anybody realise what he was up to. He walked up to the plant, said 'that's a lovely thing' then ran his hand down it!"

Aveyard laughed. "Ouch!" he said.

"We've sent Constable Everett to see Mr Bage. The two of 'em can have a field day with the tweezers!" Inspector Coates turned the pages of the Incidents Book. "One more thing," he said, his voice solemn, "they've completed the analysis of the arsenic in the hypodermic, and the stuff in the greenhouse. There were three samples. A and B, and C which appears to be a mixture of A and B. C and the stuff in the hypodermic match completely. Mr Bage is willing to swear in court they are identical ..."

"It's not like Mr Bage to be so unequivocal ..."

"Three places of decimals, he quoted to me!"

"Fingerprints on the hypodermic?"

"None, but we found a pair of rubber gloves in the kitchen. According to Robinson, both wore the gloves at different times. There are smears on the hypodermic consistent with being handled by the gloves, but Mr Bage doesn't want to be quoted about that!"

"I'll bet he doesn't!" Aveyard put on his overcoat. "That meeting with the Chief Superintendent, you know it's postponed until tomorrow?" Aveyard said, checking the Incidents Book. Inspector Coates nodded. Aveyard looked at him. "You seem tired," he said. "There's no need for you to hang around here on a Sunday. You've got everything organised so well it'd run itself for a few hours. Why don't you take the rest of the day off, come in tomorrow. We can always get you at home if we have a real crisis ..."

"She'll have me planting daffodils! I'm late with 'em already. But if I'm not there, she'll talk the lad into doing 'em ..."

"You'd rather be here than in the garden?"

"In November? The ground'll be soaking. Let the lad cope for once; he's younger than I am and hasn't felt his first rheumatism yet!"

Aveyard turned to go. "You want to open a window," he said, "or you'll all be gassed by this cigarette smoke! When Sergeant Bruton comes in, ask him to put anything he's got into the book. I imagine he'll want to take a hand in checking the Flying Fox, knowing him, though Division won't thank him. If anybody wants me, if anybody kills anybody else, you'll find me at the Western house, looking at plants."


The cottage John Western had bought was on Tunnet Lane, south of East Lodge Farm. Built of brown ironstone, it had been four workers' cottages in the days when farming was done by horse and hand. Time was when East Lodge provided work for six men; every hedge on the farm was layered by hand, and birds found food and refuge in the fruiting brambles, elderberries, and woody nightshade. Now Bill Hopton drives a tractor along the side of his fields and chops the few remaining hedges with a power-drive circular saw two feet in diameter; you can go all day without seeing a bird or a berry. One man in the beast yard milks all the cows by electric suction while they listen wide-eyed to radio pop; once each cow had a name; now their ears are tagged with a rust-proof metal number plate and the milk yield recorded on a punched paper tape that can condemn a cow to the butcher if the feed yield ratio figures dip below the line.

John Western saw the four farm cottages up for sale; he'd fallen in love with the hues of the ironstone and bought the lot. He knocked down some of the interior walls to make a sizeable country dwelling. A previous tenant had installed a greenhouse; John noticed self-sown plants growing in it, which eventually turned into delicious tomatoes. The extension into cactus growing followed a meeting with the Collis's of Finedon, and a visit to their outstanding display.

Superintendent Aveyard came out of the school and, on instinct turned right up Tingdene Way. It would soon be Sunday lunch-time; already he could smell cooking from some of the houses he passed. Small windows, set in varnished wood; glimpses of the low beamed rooms inside, women wearing pinafores, arranging the table. Ornaments gleamed, horse brasses on leathers over the mantelpiece, timbers shone with elbow grease and wax, the cat sat on the mat, dad in the cretonne covered chair, glancing at the Sunday newspaper prior to reading it later in the day, old hands holding the football pages, shaking their heads over teams falsely predicted to win on the week's football pools coupon.

He passed three people on the way up the street; gave three cheery good mornings, received three 'watch it, here's the law!' glances. He felt like a headmaster, walking through a school playground; a Constable, a Sergeant, even an Inspector, they are acceptable; 'there but for the grace of God go I', the people think. But he was a Superintendent; Constables, Sergeants, and Inspectors were answerable to *him*! Like a priest, a prostitute, a judge or a tax-collector, he had become one of *them*! Different professionally and inhuman.

In Tunnet Lane he turned left, ducked suddenly into the shade of a tree.

John Western was walking down the side of Benny Latham's house, as if he'd just come out of the back-door. He paused when he came to the front of the house, gave a quick look up and down Tunnet Lane before stepping out and hurrying towards his own house, about a hundred and fifty yards away on the same side as Benny's.

Aveyard stayed where he was, beneath the tree. Why would John Western go into Latham's cottage? What could they possibly have in common? Why the back door? Why be cautious when he came out? Aveyard had seen that type of exit many times, that pause, quick look up and down. John Western hadn't wanted it known he had been in Benny Latham's house; but why not?

"That's a good looking cactus," he said, when he stood in front of it, John Western at his side.

"How about these chrysanthemums!" Western said, pride in his voice. "Not bad for an amateur, are they?"

"You must have green fingers! Where do you buy your ... what do you grow them from, seeds, cuttings ...? Get 'em from Benny Latham, do you? I believe he does a nice line in chrysanthemums, from what I've been told ..."

"There you have me, Superintendent. I suppose I ought to confess!"

"About what, Mr Western, Benny Latham ...?"

"Good Lord no; the chrysanthemums. I bought 'em in Birton, in pots ... To do the job properly, you have to strike your own cuttings. I haven't reached that standard yet!"

"I prefer the cactus, myself. Pity it's damaged ... How did that happen?" Aveyard eyed the bench on which the cactus stood, three feet high. Above the bench was a plank, supported on two wire cross ties. On the plank were a number of flower pots. "Don't tell me," he said, "let me guess. You were reaching up on to that plank to get down a flower pot, the pot was cracked, and it fell out of your hands and damaged the cactus ..."

Western laughed. "I snapped a chrysanthemum once like that, but that wasn't how the cactus got damaged ..."

Aveyard waited. No more was forthcoming. "Want to tell me how it happened?" he said finally, his voice quiet. This was a moment he recognised. How many times had he been questioning a man and suddenly reached the point at which the man decides whether to lie or tell the truth. A policeman's got a seventh sense for lies. "It might help us in our investigations to know exactly how that cactus was damaged ..." he said. There was no reply.

"When was it damaged, can you tell me that?"

"Thursday evening, about eight o'clock, if you want me to be precise!"

"Before the Bonfire? Where were you Thursday night?"

"I was here. In the house, out here in the greenhouse, down at the pub, back home, bed about twelve o'clock ..."

"Do you sleep alone?"

"Why? Why are you asking a question like that?"

"If you sleep with your wife, she'd know where you are all night, wouldn't she?"

"I sleep on my own ..."

"Own room, or single beds in the same room?"

"Look, Superintendent ..."

"No, you look, Mr Western. I'm investigating two murders. There's a cactus connected in those murders; we don't yet know how and why, but that cactus was damaged. And you have a damaged cactus. It may be that whoever put that corpse on the Bonfire did so during the night. My best guess would be that, if the Guy was changed, it happened during Thursday night. I want to know where you were on Thursday night, Mr Western."

"All right," Western said. "I sleep on my own, in a separate room. I'm what you'd call a noisy sleeper, apparently. I snore and cough and generally make life hell for my wife. Now, as to the cactus, well, when we arrived from London on Thursday night, we had our house guest with us. I nipped out here to water my plants, and my wife followed me out. I'd been working hard all the week on a mural that had to be finished by Thursday for hanging. We hadn't seen much of each other all week; I'd been painting most nights. We, well, you know, Superintendent, you're a grown man ...!"

"There was what you might call horse-play, and the cactus got knocked over ...?"

"Don't let Jeanne hear you calling it horse-play ..."

Both of them laughed, the tension partly relieved.

"But you were alone all night?" Aveyard insisted.

"Jeanne had cactus spines in her back. I had to use the tweezers on her! By the time I got out all the spines we were

155

so tired we fell asleep in the same bed together."

Any other police officer would have left it at that, but not Aveyard. "As I was walking along Tunnet Lane to come to see you, I saw you coming out of Mr Latham's cottage. Would you care to tell me what you were doing there ...?"

"Look, Superintendent," Western said, "this has gone far enough. I'm prepared to reveal intimate details of my life with my wife to you, because I can see that might help you in your enquiries, but what I was doing in Latham's cottage has absolutely nothing to do with *you*, and I refuse to answer questions about it. I've got to draw the line somewhere, and so have you! I don't want to become all pompous and start talking about the rights of the individual, but you have no cause to interrogate me about my relationships with other people, unless those people are directly concerned in the crime you're investigating and you can prove that to me, or you have reasonable grounds to suspect that I've committed a crime. In which case, you ought to arrest me!"

"Somebody's been selling do-it-yourself police law books in this village!" Aveyard said as he left.

# CHAPTER TWENTY-FIVE

"We don't do catering usually on a Sunday," Esther Larrapin said, "but I can manage you a hot beef sandwich if that's all right?"

Aveyard had gone to the pub when he left John Western. The bar was crowded. Benny Latham was standing at one end, a pint in front of him. It wasn't his first. He nodded when the superintendent came in, but they didn't speak. The two Bollard boys and Iris Latham were playing darts, Aubrey dressed in a sober Sunday suit, Jimmy wearing fashionable levies and an undervest buttoned at the neck with short sleeves, that once had belonged to his grandfather and on which his sister Daphne had splashed dyes of various hues. He was wearing square cut 'sun' glasses with a steel frame, the glass light blue. Around his wrist he wore a thick stainless steel identification chain. Dodson Bragg was standing by the bar with Greaves and Arthur Tewson; Hopton and Coulson were sitting on the bench beneath the window, not talking other than in monosyllables. Herbert Larrapin was chatting across the bar to the American, Julian Muller.

"How is it going, Superintendent?" Julian said when Aveyard had ordered a drink, "or shouldn't I ask?"

"It all takes time. I'm not dissatisfied!"

Esther came back with his sandwich. "I hope you've saved some of that beef for me!" Herbert said in mock horror.

"Aye, you look as if you need it!" she replied, "you're getting a stomach on you as if you were six months gone!"

"Mr Western not with you?" Aveyard asked Julian Muller, casually.

"I've been for a walk round the village. I thought I'd drop in here on the way back. I imagine he's at home!"

"He *was* in," Herbert said, "looked in when we opened, gulped one down, and left! But that's regular with him, once a month! Regular as clockwork. In when we open, half a pint, then gone!"

"Anybody else in, then?"

"Only Benny. He's always here when we open, and young Jimmy there, him playing darts in the fancy glasses! Your Sergeant's been in," he said, "said he was looking for you! We made him stop and sup half a pint, since you've got the poor sod working on a Sunday. By the way," he said, "here's a bit of news for you. I don't know if you've found anything out yet about that lad on the Bonfire, but one thing I can tell you. It wasn't Brian Sharp! He was in here not twenty minutes ago, collecting his keys! He's back, from London!"

Esther Larrapin had gone to the cubby hole to answer the telephone; she put the instrument down and came along the bar. "There's a telephone call for you, Superintendent!" He excused himself, walked along the bar, reached over and grasped the receiver. "Can you manage all right?" Esther asked. He nodded. "Superintendent Aveyard," he said.

"Inspector Coates."

"I'm in a bar ..."

"I thought you might want to know. They've fished the spines out of Everett's hand. They come from the same type of plant as the spines in the dead man's hand!"

"Bage is certain?"

"Absolutely!"

"Same type?"

"That's what he says."

"But he won't confirm it's the same?"

"No! I pressed him. He got quite shirty. He wants the plant. Not that he thinks he'll be able to find anything from it. You've seen Western?"

"Yes! Sergeant Bruton get on to London?"

"Yes, they've put teams out for us, Petticoat Lane, Portobello Road, King's Road. They're not very hopeful ..."

"Neither am I!"

"He's seen Olive Abbott, and there's something I want to talk to *you* about. When are you coming in?"

"Right now. You had lunch? Can I bring you a hot beef sandwich?"

"I wish I'd waited! We had a plate of chop suey and noodles from the Chinese Restaurant in Pirton. That and Curry Sam's is the only place open on a Sunday! Who'd be a policeman!"

"Which would you rather—plant wet daffodils, or eat cold chop suey?"

# CHAPTER TWENTY-SIX

The postponed meeting was suddenly reinstated; Superintendent Aveyard and Sergeant Bruton arrived at the office of the Chief Constable shortly after the Chief Detective Superintendent. "This is just an informal meeting," the Chief Constable said but no-one was deceived by that; he wanted to know everything, to look at everything, and woe-betide them if any piece of paper, any document however unimportant, was missing. Bruton showed him the book of photographs. "Not much to go on there," the Chief Constable said, handing them to the Chief. He skimmed through the statements. "Too many eye-witnesses," he said. Aveyard went through the crimes methodically, needing to refer to Sergeant Bruton only occasionally on a matter of detail. When he had finished his recital, the Chief Constable looked at the Chief.

"Well, what do *you* think?" he asked.

"It's an odd case, with a lot of strange elements. I agree with the basic line the Superintendent is taking though it's too early to see any connection between the Robinson case and the Bonfire case. I don't think he'll be able to connect the pheasant poaching, and the petty thieving; but I agree he should investigate them all simultaneously."

"Do you think Robinson killed his wife?"

"He had the motive and opportunity!"

"But took no steps to evade arrest?"

"He could be playing it clever. After all, he's got away with it twice before ..."

The Chief Constable ruffled through the papers. "We have sufficient evidence to charge him!"

"With what we've got, and unless Bill can come up with something else, we have no alternative but to charge him. We shall have to try to discover where he bought that hypodermic, but I'm not optimistic about a positive identification. You can buy them over the counter in any chemists, as long as you say it's for a diabetic ... Of course, finding it in the chair complicates the case. The defence is bound to ask, why put it in the chair? He had plenty of opportunity, presumably, since she was his own wife, to put his knee into the small of her back and hold her while he stuck it in."

"Any thoughts about the corpse on the Bonfire?"

"I can't see the connection, yet, between that and the village. Certainly there's nobody missing in the village now this chap Brian Sharp has turned up again. And if anybody from the village had killed somebody from another parish, I can't see 'em bringing the body back home to put on the Bonfire."

"Why 'on the Bonfire'?" the Chief Constable said. "That worries me. Why put it on the Bonfire? Assume it was put there during the night. Anybody could have come along while they were dragging the real Guy down, stripping the clothing off it, substituting a body, sewing the clothing back on ..."

Sergeant Bruton coughed. "With permission, sir?" he said. "I showed a sample of the clothing in which the victim was wrapped to Mrs Olive Abbott. Mr Bage had compared a sample of her sewing with the sewing on the Guy, and both were similar in style. Olive Abbott identified the stitching positively. Mr Bage is of the opinion the clothing was never unstitched ..."

"Which leaves us only two possibilities. Either Olive Abbott sewed the dead man into the clothing, and I think we're all agreed that is inconceivable, or the clothing was taken apart in a way that left the original stitching intact ..." the Chief Constable said.

"But why?" Superintendent Aveyard shook his head. "We keep coming back to this thought. Why put the body on the Bonfire? Why, since we seem to have proved that changing the clothing must have been hazardous and complicated, why do it?"

"Disposal of the body is always the major matter in any murder case, we all know that," the Chief said, thinking out loud. They all nodded agreement. "We've been assuming, haven't we, that the murderer—and that itself is an assumption

—the person responsible for the disposal of that body had freedom of choice. We've assumed they could decide whether to bury the body, to dismember it, to drop it into the gravel pit, or incinerate it, any one of the classic methods of disposal. But what if whoever needed to dispose of that body had no other alternative?" He looked at their mystified faces. "We ought to try to work out a set of circumstances in which the disposer had no alternative but to place the body on the Bonfire ..."

The Chief Constable looked around. "I don't think there's anything more we can do today; we'll think about what the Chief Detective Superintendent has said, and compare notes at a meeting first thing in the morning. Now, gentlemen, if you'll excuse me, I have a motor car engine waiting for me ..."

"And I have half a dozen roses to plant ..." the Chief added.

"Before we end the meeting," Superintendent Aveyard asked, "what's the deadline for arresting Stanley Robinson? At the moment he's 'helping with enquiries' ..."

"Let's leave it like this. Unless you get in touch with the Chief and give him good reason why he shouldn't do so, he'll arrest Stanley Robinson on suspicion of murder at twelve o'clock tomorrow; the papers will go to the public prosecutor's office tomorrow afternoon."

Aveyard and Bruton rode back to Ulton in companionable silence, both considering what the Chief had said. Fresh mind, fresh approach. The Chief might have something, but what would make placing the corpse on the Bonfire inevitable ...?

Aveyard left the car in the village; Bruton continued in it to the Flying Fox. Pheasant was not on the menu. The Italian, Giovanni, was responsible for most of the purchases. Yes, he bought the pheasants. Where did they come from? They were delivered. Nothing wrong with 'em, was there? They bought, and paid for 'em in good faith. Not 'bent' were they? "Hang on a minute," Giovanni said, "I have the latest receipt here, somewhere." He rummaged among the papers in the tiny office adjoining the kitchen of the restaurant, which looked like a battlefield after the fifty or more lunches they'd prepared and served. Bruton looked about him. It seemed impossible the order of a plate of food would come from such a chaos of pans and dishes and food scraps. Giovanni caught his eye. "You'd never believe it could be done, would you?" he said. "On a busy night we can cater for more than a hundred, every plateful different!"

"Including pheasant ...?"

Giovanni passed the receipt to him. It was printed, and perforated down one side, obviously torn from a receipt book. 'PHEASANT FARMERS,' the heading said, the 'Birton' the only address. 'Received from' then the name of the restaurant 'THE FLYING FOX', entered in capital letters with a biro pen, the amount, and a scrawled signature. Pheasant was sixty new pence a portion on the menu; The Flying Fox was paying its supplier a pound a bird, that would make at least four portions, more if you added the pheasant casserole at forty new pence a portion, and the game bird soup at twenty new pence a helping.

"Can you read the signature?" the Sergeant asked.

Giovanni scrutinised it. "Can't say I can! I never thought to try."

"What's the address of Pheasant Farmers?"

"To be honest with you, I don't know. I believe he comes from Birton. I understand he supplies all the restaurants. Grows the birds himself, you know ... They've never been shot."

"Or picks 'em up ..."

"Poaching? I don't believe it. I mean, he was in a regular way of business, little van, printed letter-heads, receipts, all above board."

"This little van, can you describe it?"

"A mini, just an ordinary mini ..."

"Anything painted on the side of it?"

"Well, now you come to mention it, no, I mean, it was just a plain van. I never thought of it that way ..."

"People never do," Sergeant Bruton said bitterly. "Just because a man comes in a van with something printed on a piece of paper, you believe he is a legitimate business man. He didn't turn up this week, right?"

"No, he didn't. Let us down badly. He'd guaranteed regular supplies; that's why we had it on the permanent menu not the 'specials of the day'."

"He's been delivering for a long time ..."

"We start pheasant first week in September ..."

163

"But pheasant shooting doesn't start legally until the first of October ...?"

"Big demand for game these days. We used to keep them in the freezer but the taste went. Now we buy them from places that hatch them early. Tame birds, but the taste is there. We don't get much demand in the summer, but come September first, when the evenings start to draw in ..."

"And you don't know the name of the man who was supplying 'em?"

"I suppose he must have told me his name at the start, but even after all these years, I still can't remember English names."

Sergeant Bruton took out his notebook. "All right," he said disgustedly, "let's start from the beginning. What does he look like ...?"

The printer confirmed the description; he hadn't enjoyed being woken from an after-lunch doze, any more than the police driver had enjoyed adding yet another two hours to his already long working week. Grumbling, the printer opened the tiny works attached to his house.

"What address did he give?" Bruton asked.

"He didn't give me one."

"When did you do the job?"

"Here we are, July 25th two hundred sheets, printed, perforated and bound. No, there's no address, but there wouldn't be. It says here, 'to be collected'. He must have come for them himself!"

"Anybody can walk in here, call themselves anything, and you'll print cards, letterheads, invoices, anything. No address, no telephone number. You want your head examining!"

"Now see here, Sergeant. There's nothing in the law that says I have to play the detective. I make my living printing. It's no crime. If you don't like what we do, then change the law, don't come waking me up on a Sunday afternoon expecting me to have done your job for you!"

"All right," Sergeant Bruton said, "keep your shirt on."

The printer was right, of course. There was no point in blaming him for a loop-hole in the law which permitted any rascal with money in his hand to order virtually any printing except bank notes and lottery coupons. Thank God the printer put his own name on his work, or they'd never have found him!

"Where's the Superintendent?" he asked when he got back to the Incidents Room, "and you'd better let that driver have time off—he's been grinding gears like a coffee machine all the way back from Birton! And damn near drove through a stop sign!"

Inspector Coates grinned. "You've had the rough edge of somebody's tongue at a guess ..."

When Sergeant Bruton finished writing in the Incidents Book, he handed Inspector Coates two completed standard report forms. The Inspector read them, whistled softly.

"It'll break the Super's heart," Sergeant Bruton said, "he'd taken that lad under his wing, thought he could do no wrong!"

"We better set up an identity parade for tomorrow ..."

The description of the man who'd delivered the pheasants and of the man who'd ordered the printing, tallied exactly. Either could have been Benny Latham. Superintendent Aveyard walked into the Incidents Room and the telephone rang on his desk before he'd even had time to say hello. He picked it up, listened to the voice on the other end, then beckoned to Sergeant Bruton and Inspector Coates both to pick up the extensions on the desks they were using.

"Inspector Hardcastle, here, from 4 Division of the Metropolitan Police. Your Sergeant Bruton called us this morning, and made a certain enquiry ..."

"This is Superintendent Aveyard. I have Sergeant Bruton on an extension. Have you found anything ...?"

"Well, when the Sergeant telephoned, he asked for certain enquiries to be made, and though some of the locations were not in this Division, I took it upon myself to co-ordinate enquiries in the Metropolitan area ..."

"We're very grateful," Aveyard said, grimacing at Sergeant Bruton. "May I ask if you've found anything ..."

"The objects we were called upon to seek were ..."

"I know what the objects were, Inspector. I'm afraid time is pressing at this end and I'd be grateful ..."

"I have the list here ..." Sergeant Bruton said, placing it in front of the Superintendent.

"We have a copy of the list. Can you tell me about any one

of the objects. This glass case containing moths and butterflies for example. Have you found anything like that?"

"No, nothing like that. We found many cases of butterflies, of course, some of which were most attractive, but they were all without exception every one of them, taller and greater in diameter than the one you described to us ..."

Aveyard placed his hand over the mouthpiece of the telephone. "If he goes through the whole list, one by one," he said to Bruton, "it'll take him an hour!"

"Sergeant Bruton here, Inspector. I'm the chap who called originally. That set of handbells, number on the list ..."

"Yes, we think we've got them ..."

"Any inscription?"

"Yes, barely legible though. They must have been cleaned a hundred ..."

"Ulton Parish Church, 1874, Stedman Caters, five hours fifteen minutes, June 14th ...?"

"Well, there seems to be some doubt about the date. Looking at it, you can't be certain if ..."

"One locket, item six?"

"Well, there you have me; of course, a locket is hard ..."

"One tin, Queen Victoria Coronation ..."

"Oh yes, we have that. Quite a memory that brings back. The side of the tin is ..."

"Same stall as the bells ..."

"Yes, we have three items we think we can safely hazard a guess, and surmise are similar to the ones on your list, and all from the same stall in the Portobello Road."

"What's the stall owner say ...?"

"Well, of course, at first, I mean when we started, he didn't have a lot to say ..."

Aveyard took his hand away from the mouthpiece. "Superintendent Aveyard here, Inspector," he said, emphasising both ranks. "Did you get a description of the man reported to have sold those items to the stall holder, did you get the reported date of purchase and sale, and if so would you please read them at dictation speed, starting now."

The date of purchase came first. Friday, the fifth of November. The description which followed matched the one they'd had from Giovanni and the Printer. Benny Latham, to a 'T'!

Sergeant Bruton groaned. Superintendent Aveyard, thoughtful, put down his extension, leaving Inspector Coates to carry on the conversation with London. "It's not possible," he said, "it's just not possible. Benny Latham wasn't in London on November 5th."

"We don't *know* that," Sergeant Bruton said. "We've never asked him. He could have gone up there and back, day trip. Catch the 10.25, he'd be in London 11.40. Tube to the Portobello Road, quick sale, since he's been doing it for years to judge from the amount of stuff missing. Back to St Pancras in time for the 12.30. He'd be inside his cottage at a quarter past two!"

"You'll go see him, will you Jim?" Aveyard asked, disappointment in his voice.

"There's also the matter of the pheasants. It's in the book. The Italian at The Flying Fox, and a printer in Birton, the descriptions are right. It could be Benny. We were going to set up an identification parade, tomorrow ... with your permission and approval of course."

Aveyard shook his head from side to side. "That devil," he said, "he took me in. I believed him last night. I've already written a report for the Chief Constable, asking for an enquiry into Latham's accusation of persecution. Go and see him for me, Jim. I'm not sure I could keep my hands off him!"

"I wanted to tell you about my meeting with Olive Abbott. Something odd there. It's in the book ..."

"That can wait. See Benny Latham for me, and if you get a cough from him that he was on that train, take him to Birton. Whatever you do, don't bring him in here, to me!"

Bruton left; Superintendent Aveyard prowled round the schoolroom, furious, looking over the shoulders of the girls typing reports and statements, the Sergeant working the copying machine, the Divisional Detective Constables, writing their reports.

"Here you are, Superintendent," the girl who'd been on duty the previous night said, handing him a plastic carton of tea from the machine. He took it from her, murmured thanks, then stood surveying the room while he drank it. "It's all there, somewhere!" he thought. Inspector Coates was on the telephone, still taking the report from London. Goods stolen in the village, taken up to London for selling. By whom? The description said Benny Latham. Pheasants being stolen, sold to The Flying Fox. By whom? The description again said, Benny Latham. A corpse found on a Bonfire. Who was it—and again the connection, Benny Latham; he's the lad tied it there with barbed wire. John Western has a damaged cactus, and was seen coming from the cottage of whom—Benny Latham. The Superintendent had watched that with his own eyes. Damn it, the only event in the village in which Benny Latham didn't figure was the Helen Robinson death. It was all there, in the Incidents Book, somewhere.

Inspector Coates put down the telephone. "At last, Superintendent," he said, "now we can have that talk."

"Make out your report, first! You've warned that garrulous twit in London we'll need the stall holder for identification?" Inspector Coates nodded. It wasn't like the Superintendent to run down a junior police officer, even though Coates himself had the same rank. He had started transcribing the notes he had taken during the telephone call when Harry Greaves came in. "Could I have a word with you?" Harry Greaves said.

"I'm a bit busy. Could the Sergeant help?"

Superintendent Aveyard overheard. "Can I help you, Mr Greaves, isn't it?" he asked. He led the way into the small classroom in which he'd interrogated Benny Latham the previous night. "It's difficult to know exactly what to do, especially on a Sunday since I can't get anybody at Head Office, but I thought you ought to know ..." Harry Greaves said.

"Ought to know what?"

"You know I'm the village postmaster?"

"Yes?"

"There's only one delivery in the village. Every morning."

"Yes?"

"I'm sorry to go such a long way about it, but it's important you have the full background. There's two post-boxes in the village. One outside the shop, one in Ulton Lane, at the end of Eastfields. They're cleared at nine o'clock each morning. Well, nine o'clock down Eastfields, five minutes past at the shop."

"What do you do with the letters in the post-boxes?"

"I sort 'em. Any that might be local, I put to one side. Any out of the village, I hand 'em over to the van man when he comes, about half-past-nine. There were forty-two local ones yesterday morning, that's like Saturday morning. Mostly they were circulars the vicar had sent out, being returned. Now, seeing as it's Saturday, and there's no post of a Sunday morning, I lock the letters up in the safe. Then, come Sunday afternoon when I've postmarked 'em I get 'em out of the safe, and sort 'em out, ready for delivery on Monday morning. I also add to 'em any that have been put in the box on Sunday morning. When I came to sort the mail this afternoon, I found a letter. I think you ought to know about it."

"What's special about it, Mr Greaves?"

"It's in Helen Robinson's handwriting ..."

"And it was posted, when?"

"Sometime between last post Friday, and nine o'clock Saturday morning."

"You're certain it's Mrs Robinson, the deceased Mrs Robinson's handwriting?"

"Positive."

"Why are you so positive?"

"She's one of ... I should say, she *was* one of the few people in Eastfields who shopped with me. Most of 'em go to Birton, you know. But she gave me an order every week; I gave her a book to write it in, and the handwriting's identical. I'd swear to that. Handwriting's a bit of a hobby with me ..."

"We can always compare them scientifically. They analyse the inks as well as the style of the writing. May I have the letter?"

"That's what's so awkward," Harry Greaves said. "I've never met anything like this, and I wanted to refer to Head Office. I'm not sure I'm right even disclosing to a third party there is such a letter in existence. I can't hand it over. It's drummed into us by Head Office that a letter entrusted to the post office is sacred. We can't do any other than deliver the letter ..."

"Even though it may be the last letter written by a woman later discovered dead, in suspicious circumstances ..."

"I know. That's what makes it awkward ... I'm obliged to

169

deliver the letter to the person to whom it's addressed. I'm sorry, Superintendent, but I'm afraid that's what I must do ..."

"One thing you can tell me, Mr Greaves, whose name is on the envelope ..."

Harry Greaves held the letter so the Superintendent could see the front of it. "I'm afraid I can't tell you who the letter is addressed to, Superintendent," he said. The name was quite clear, in a round obviously womanish hand. Mr Benny Latham, Tunnet Lane, Ulton.

# CHAPTER TWENTY-SEVEN

Mr Bage rang. Even though Inspector Coates said the Superintendent had someone with him, Mr Bage insisted on being put through. Harry Greaves said he was leaving anyway. "Though it's not usual on a Sunday, I shall deliver this letter this afternoon, Superintendent," he said, "to Benny Latham in person at four o'clock. Any idea where Benny might be at that time?"

"Sitting at that desk! I want to be there when that letter's opened!"

The Superintendent picked up the telephone. "Yes, Mr Bage," he said.

"You know Stanley Robinson's been taking arsenic in small doses for months ...?"

"Yes, Doctor Samson told me ..."

"I know how he's been getting it ..."

"Like I've always said, you're a genius!"

"People have strange habits. Gardeners, for instance. Taking his tea every morning, in the greenhouse. He'd made up a mixture ..."

"Sergeant Bruton told me. Exhibit C I believe you've labelled it ...?"

"Yes. The mixture formed itself into lumps. He broke the lumps with a piece of cane. What do you think he stirred his tea with every morning?"

"Let me guess. The same piece of cane ...?"

"That's right!"

"Well, all I can say is, he wants his head examining!"

"Of course he washed the cane and wiped it dry every time he used it for arsenic. When we found it—it's exhibit C/2 by the way and the jar of mixture is C/1—it was quite clean. But he forgot one feature of garden canes ..."

"And that is ...?"

"Ask any earwig! They're hollow. There was enough arsenic jammed up the hollow to kill a regiment!"

"... of earwigs!"

"There was enough to make certain that, every morning, he was stirring sufficient into his cup of tea eventually to kill himself!"

# CHAPTER TWENTY-EIGHT

Benny Latham reported to the Village School a little before four o'clock, in the company of Sergeant Bruton. Superintendent Aveyard had asked the Chief Superintendent to be there, since there might be trouble about the letter. They put Latham into the small classroom while they listened to Bruton's report. "I'm afraid he's clean as a whistle," Sergeant Bruton said. "Well, so far as the London trip's concerned. We have separate identifications for him more or less at hourly intervals throughout the day. Harry Greaves at the shop; apparently Benny went in to buy some things his wife wanted; Larrapin at the pub, and Tom Coulson, who was also in the pub. The last one, and I suppose he's unimpeachable, is the Reverend Francis Elks. He was talking to Benny at three o'clock!"

"So he didn't go to London on Friday?"

"We can be certain of that!"

"But we have a description that matches him exactly ..."

"Yes, right down to the cap he wears!"

The Chief Superintendent had been listening. "That chap Brian Sharp. We suspect he was in London over the weekend. I understand he's not yet been seen ...?"

"I was going to see him myself ..."

"Let one of the Constables see him, one who hasn't had much to do with Benny Latham. At this stage you only want to know where Sharp spent the week-end. Let a Constable ask him, and when he gets back, ask the Constable for a description."

Aveyard looked at his Chief. "Something up your sleeve, Chief? Something we don't know about?"

"Only an idea. These villages are self-contained. Not so much nowadays, of course, when everybody has an old banger; but I remember once, when I was investigating a case in a village like this one, oh, it's years ago now, but we had a problem of identity. If you scratch back two or three generations, you'll find all these lads come from the same stock, and share the same physical characteristics …"

"We know there's a stock type in the womenfolk," Sergeant Bruton said, "they talk about *the Ulton Lumps*, short fat women …"

"That could be why you keep on getting the same description, and because you have a picture of Benny Latham in your mind, they all seem to be him …"

"Well, it's true I mistook Roger Blatsoe for Benny that night we were staking out the grounds of the Hall …" Aveyard said.

"I don't want to interfere, but what I'd do if I were you," the Chief said, "is give that description to the detectives who've conducted the interrogations. You'll be surprised how many different 'recognitions' you'll get!"

When Sergeant Bruton had arranged for that to be done, they went into the room where Benny Latham was waiting. His eyes glittered at them. "Didn't take you long to go over to the other side," he said accusingly at Aveyard. "I fooled myself you wasn't going to be like all the others!"

Harry Greaves had been waiting outside. He came in when Aveyard beckoned. "I've got a letter here," he said, "it's for you, Benny!"

"Why don't you shove it through the letter box?"

"Because I want evidence of delivery …" He held out the letter, but Benny Latham didn't take it.

"I don't know as I want it," he said. "I allus thought as a man and his letters was private. Why don't you shove it through the letter box, in the usual way. I know you lot; you've got nothing on me, and I'm not touching that letter. Until that letter drops through my letter box onto my mat, it's got nothing to do with me …"

"It's got your name on it," Aveyard said.

"How do you know that, *Superintendent*? I don't know as there's anything in the book o' rules that gives you a right to look at my letters afore I do!"

"I haven't looked at it. From where I'm now standing I can see the postmaster holding a letter with your name on it. Now do us all a favour, including yourself, and take that letter from Mr Greaves!"

"He doesn't have to take it," the Chief Superintendent said. "Nothing says he has to handle it. You're quite within your right, postmaster, to place that envelope on the desk in front of him. That would constitute a 'delivery'."

"Oh, I'm not sure about that," Harry Greaves said, worried. "We can't just put the mail down anywhere," he said. "I think I'm obliged to do as he asks, and take the letter up to his house and put it through the letter box ... Oh dear, I wish it wasn't Sunday. I wish I could have talked to Head Office about all this ..."

Benny Latham looked from one to the other. "Got you again, haven't I?" he said.

Aveyard had been standing. He seated himself on the desk behind him. "Yes, you have," he said. "You've got us, and we've got you! Stalemate! It's Sunday afternoon, and we'd all be better employed doing other things, but here we are, playing games again. I don't blame you; believe it or not, I meant what I said the other night. You're a man with a chip on his shoulder, and it's my job to see how justified that chip is. Let me say this quite clearly to you. Even if we put you inside for the rest of your life as a result of our present investigations, I shall still investigate your charge of persecution, and if I can find it's justified, I shall make a full report to my Chief, and I know he'll want to do something about it!"

The Chief nodded; though he didn't speak.

"One; we've got a description of the lad who's been flogging pheasants to The Flying Fox, and it matches the way you look. It could be, mind you I'm only saying *could be* at the moment, a description of you. But it's enough to give me cause to detain you, and bring you before an identification parade tomorrow. Two, we've got a description of a lad who's been stealing stuff in this village, and then again, that *could be* you, but I couldn't arrest you for that because we've taken the trouble to prove, *we've* proved, not you, that you couldn't have been in London when the sales were made. We believe the contents of that letter might help us solve the problem of Helen Robinson. We'd like your co-operation. You can help us, by taking that letter, opening it, and then answering a few questions about the contents. I don't want to pry into your private affairs, unless they are specifically concerned with a crime. Now, will you help us?"

"You're the first copper hasn't threatened me at the end of a speech like that," Benny Latham said, as he took the envelope from Harry Greaves, who looked relieved. "You don't need me any more, do you?" he asked anxiously. Aveyard shook his head, still looking at Benny Latham as if to hold on to the fine thread of confidence he had established. Harry Greaves left the room. Benny Latham was looking at the envelope. "You're right enough about one thing," he said, "it's from Helen. She must 'a posted it last thing Friday night, I suppose, and the next morning, she was dead."

"You knew her well?" Aveyard asked quietly.

"Not the way you dirty minded buggers are thinking," he said, defiant.

"I never said anything about that."

"I know what you're thinking. What's a man like me got in common with a lass her age? Oh, she was flighty. I've listened to 'em in the pub, but I held my peace. To hear 'em talk she spent half her young life on her back ..."

"But she wasn't like that?"

"Not with me, any road!" Benny Latham said. He put his thumb under the flap of the envelope and tore it open. There were two pages in the envelope, covered in ball-point writing, smeared a little.

"That's probably the last thing she ever said to anybody other than her husband," Aveyard said.

Benny Latham didn't read the letter. He folded it again, put it back into the envelope. Aveyard watched him. 'Careful, careful!' He prayed neither the Chief nor the Sergeant would speak, silently he cursed himself for having them present at this interview. Benny could go two ways. Stubborn, he could destroy the envelope and its contents. That was his privilege. Or he could hand it over. That was his 'duty'; but were the effects of police antipathy ingrained in him? It would be an exquisite revenge after all these years to stand on his rights and refuse to help.

"You'll want my fingerprints," Benny Latham said, "to compare. I imagine you've got hers. She used to come and sit beside me in the pub; she talked to me, like a human being. She was the only one. The rest of 'em treated me like muck but she never did. She was a lovely person," he said, and handed the envelope to Superintendent Aveyard with the last letter of Helen Robinson intact inside it.

"We'll photocopy it, and let you have it back right away," Aveyard said.

Benny Latham shook his head. "I don't want to see it," he said, "I don't ever want to know what's inside it."

Dear Benny,

You know I don't like coming round, because people do talk so. But you've always been kind to me. Well, Benny, I've had a row with Brian. You always did tell me no good would come of it, and it looks as if you're proving yourself right. He's not the same as he was ever since I told him about the baby. Well, today when he was round here, supposed to be fixing Stanley's chair, we had a row. He said as he loves me, but he can't go on what with me living with Stanley and everything, and him lying in bed at nights thinking about me and Stanley doing it. Well, I've told him time and time again we don't do it any more so he has no cause to be jealous but I can't bring myself to leave Stanley just yet, I just can't bring myself to do it to him. So what I was wondering, Benny, was, since Brian seems to listen to you, if you'd talk with him and tell him calm down and hang on a bit. He knows I love him dearly and I'll leave Stanley in my own time when I can bring myself to do it without breaking his heart. But if you'd just talk to Brian for me, and oblige, your grateful friend,

Helen.

# CHAPTER TWENTY-NINE

"There's your motive," the Detective Chief Superintendent said. "Somehow, Stanley Robinson learned his wife was thinking of leaving him, and rather than lose her to another man, he poisoned her. A jealous husband ..."

Benny Latham had gone back to his cottage, unaccompanied. "What about them descriptions you've had, Superintendent?" he'd said, "aren't you going to arrest me?"

"If the descriptions hold water, we'll be after you. If they don't we shan't persecute you!" Aveyard had said, smiling almost for the first time since the case started.

Now they were clustered in the small room of the village school, the Detective Chief Inspector, Aveyard, Bruton, Inspector Coates, and two of the Detective Constables who'd handled the interrogations of the villagers.

"Let me paint a picture," Aveyard said to them all, "of a man called into a house on the pretext of mending a chair. The husband's away, or perhaps in his greenhouse. The chair is in the kitchen, a heavy armchair of the kind an older man uses with considerable pleasure. Young women don't sit in armchairs in the kitchen; they're too active! Our friend is fixing the chair, but for weeks past he's been consumed by jealousy at the thought his girl friend, who soon will become in the classic phrase, the mother of his child, is giving herself nightly to the older man. He's known about that chair for some time, and so he comes to the house prepared. He's brought a hypodermic, and he's taken arsenic from the greenhouse. He strips the back off the chair, and puts in the syringe. Let's face it, a girl like Helen Robinson could never have devised a fastening like that. She had no need to. There must have been a hundred occasions when her husband was asleep in bed beside her, when she could have pushed that hypo into his back. But that's not a woman's way. She'd have given him sleeping pills, arsenic in his porridge ..."

"But Mr Robinson wasn't the one poisoned," Inspector Coates reminded him.

"I know he wasn't; and that's why we're all on the wrong track. The poison wasn't meant for Helen Robinson. It was meant for the husband. That hypo was put in the chair during Friday. For one reason or another, Stanley Robinson never sat in that chair on Friday. Give me that book of photographs," he asked the Inspector. He opened the book at a photograph of the Robinsons' kitchen.

"This mark on the floor," he said. "Mr Bage proved it belonged to Mrs Robinson, and we dismissed it. But if you'll look at the footprint, you'll see it could have been caused by someone slipping. And where would they slip? Into the chair. Mrs Robinson, not a very tidy person to judge by the kitchen in general, drops bacon fat on the floor while she's cooking her husband's breakfast. He's out in the greenhouse. She steps in the bacon fat, slips backwards, and falls back into the chair. The chair that her boy friend had doctored the previous evening, ready for her husband. And the hypo goes straight into her back!"

"You'll have a job proving it!" Sergeant Bruton said. "I follow your logic, Superintendent, but I'd be a lot happier if we had a few fingerprints!"

The Chief had listened in silence. "I'll tell you where you'll get evidence," he said. "Find out what coat Brian Sharp was wearing on Friday. Ten to one he carried that hypo in his pocket at some time. And ten to one, a few drops leaked out of the end of the needle. Mr Bage'll love that. He'll give you a direct connection between the lining of that jacket, and mixture C!"

"There's a thing I want to mention," Inspector Coates said to Superintendent Aveyard, "and we haven't had a chance for a talk all morning. Reading the book, I was struck by one or two things. Put 'em side by side, and we may have something. We've been looking for a poacher, right?"

"And nobody mention B. Latham, Esq!" Aveyard said with a laugh.

"There's a man in this village with access to the birds. That

179

man's going to be out of a job quite soon, judging from the note the Superintendent has put in the book about Mr Newsome dying, based on information supplied by Dr Samson and entered here as Note 57."

"Go on!" the Chief said, good humouredly, "we all know you run a good Incidents Book; no need to boast about it!"

"What's more natural, therefore, than that the man concerned should be thinking about his future? There's a lot of money in hatching pheasants, if you go about it the right way. And there's not much employment for old gamekeepers these days!" He turned to one of the two Detective Constables. "You've heard the description we got from The Flying Fox, Arthur. Of all the people you've seen in this village, who would you say answers that description best?"

"Blatsoe. Roger Blatsoe. I questioned him about the stolen stuff. I'd say the Italian's description, and that of the printer, fits Blatsoe perfectly!"

"Thank you! I think Blatsoe was going into business for himself."

"A gamekeeper, poaching!" Aveyard said, "what next?"

Sergeant Bruton coughed. "Once again," he said, "where's the evidence?"

"An identity parade," the Chief said, "later this afternoon. That printer, and the Italian. If it is Blatsoe, they'll pick him out. I suppose he does drive a van ..."

"Yes, Chief, and it's plain grey!"

"Good!" The Chief looked round him. "Any more suggestions?" he said. "If we go on like this, we'll soon have the whole lot wrapped up. Anything else in your Incidents Book, Inspector?"

"I have something," Sergeant Bruton said, "but it's not my usual line of country; like the Inspector here, I've been trying to get a few words with the Superintendent all day, but haven't managed."

"What is it, Jim?" Aveyard asked.

"You asked me to have a chat with Olive Abbott. See if anything struck me ..."

"She hit you with a frying pan?" Inspector Coates said, relieving the tension. They all laughed.

"Olive Abbott has the appetite of a tiny bird and she's no more than skin and bone, yet if you look at the record the Superintendent gave us of his early conversation with Harry Greaves at the shop, you'll see that Olive Abbott spends a fair amount on groceries every week. Question One, who does she buy food for? Olive Abbott keeps chocolate digestive biscuits in her house, yet she doesn't eat 'em. Question two, who gets the chocolate biscuits. Question three, and this is what really got me thinking. Olive Abbott buys, and has bought for a long time, eighty cigarettes a week, yet she doesn't smoke, and there's not a single ash-tray in sight anywhere in her house ..."

"Question three, who smokes the cigarettes?" Aveyard added. "Damn it, I ought to have spotted that," he said. "I knew there was something wrong, something nagged me Saturday night when I took her home from the barn-dance. That's why I suggested you have a talk with her. But dammit, I ought to have spotted the fact there were no ash-trays ..."

"Could it be blackmail, Super?" one of the Detective Constables asked. "But instead of cash, they were doing her for groceries and cigs ...?"

"That's a possibility, though my immediate reaction is to ask, what would Olive Abbott ever have done wrong to give someone cause to blackmail her?"

"Could it be charity?" The Chief asked, throwing his idea into the melting pot. "We know she was a kindly old soul. Look at the way she bought small gifts for that boy who's gone missing, Bert Dunkley ..."

"Yes, and where has that boy got to?" Aveyard asked. They were all silent, thinking. Then three of them spoke together. "He could be in London," the Detective Constable Arthur said. "He could have fallen into the gravel pits," Inspector Coates said. "He's being hidden somewhere," Sergeant Bruton said.

Aveyard looked at the Chief, then turned to Inspector Coates. "Give me that book," he said, then, while he was turning the pages to find the one he wanted he said, "You see it too, don't you Chief?" The Chief nodded. "Olive Abbott's hiding the boy," the Chief said. "She's got him in the cellar, or the attic, pound to a penny. She's always spoiled him, according to the boy's mother, if I remember the Sergeant's deposition after he'd talked with Mrs Dunkley on the Friday night, after the lead stealing. Chocolate biscuits, that's the giveaway."

Aveyard had found the page, was reading it rapidly.

"Right," he said crisply, "action stations! Will you tackle Brian Sharp for me, Chief? Two counts; a jacket with a pocket stained with arsenic, and also the theft of articles from the village and their sale in London. Who better than a jobbing builder cum jack of all trades could go in and out of people's homes? And who was in London on Saturday. I've never seen the man, but odds on he comes as you suggested, from the same rootstock as Benny Latham, Roger Blatsoe, and a half a dozen other lads in this village!"

"I suppose you'd like a cough on both jobs ...?"

"Yes, Chief, to be frank, I would!"

"Then I'll try not to let you down. Can I take Inspector Coates with me?"

"Why not try Arthur here? See if he has the makings of a Sergeant ... Inspector Coates, you tackle Blatsoe. If he doesn't come clean, take him as far as The Flying Fox, but I don't think he'll give you any trouble ..."

"You'll find he's so meticulous," Sergeant Bruton said, remembering his visit to the Blatsoe house early Saturday morning, "he's probably kept a book of accounts ..."

"Where will you be, Superintendent?" the Chief asked, obviously pleased and impatient to be back on the job again, willing to accept the temporary command of his junior officer.

"I shall be eating chocolate digestive biscuits with a dear old lady!" he said.

# CHAPTER THIRTY

Olive Abbott by the fire stared into the flames of yesterday, today, tomorrow, who can tell what an old lady sees. The glow from the coal lit the room, pulling in its walls, reflecting off the sheen of rubbed wood, polished copper.

"Yes, he's up there," she said, "in the attic." They started to walk up the flight of steps. "If you're going up," she said, "you might take him a biscuit. He usually gets hungry about this time."

"I'm a damn fool," Aveyard said to Jim Bruton. "I ought to have seen it at once. Look at the tread of these stairs. No sign of dust. Why should she dust up here, if it was never used ...?"

They knocked on the door the way she'd told them, then, when the bolts had been withdrawn from inside, they pushed the door open. Four more stairs led into an attic, extending thirty feet long and eighteen feet wide, the entire length of the cottage, and about ten feet high in the centre. At each end was a window of frosted glass, covered with heavy curtains. Bert Dunkley sat in the chair when he saw them come up the ladder. He was pale, and his eyes had sunk into his head, but whether from apathy or resignation it would be hard to tell. Certainly he appeared to have no fear of them. All across one side of the attic floor, a model railway had been built, with track laid directly onto the random wood boards and built up cuttings and culverts and bridges. When Sergeant Bruton looked carefully, he saw that pot plants had been set in the construction, sand and soil spread to simulate the countryside. The bed was midway between the two windows, and hadn't been made for a couple of days. All over the floor were copies of the *Hotspur*, *Wizard*, *Rover* Bruton remembered from his young days, each edition eagerly awaited on the appropriate day of the week. The only story he could remember, and he thought it had been in *Hotspur*, was of an Indian called Clicky-ba, who held a bat two handed like a sledge hammer and could perform prodigious feats of strength with it, on and off the cricket field.

"Your Dad and Mum have been worried about you, lad," Aveyard said. The boy looked at him, still truculent.

He was wearing a pair of pyjama trousers, and a polo necked jumper too big for him. He hadn't washed nor combed his hair for three days and the attic was dusty.

"I'm not going back!" the boy said.

"You have to, lad," Aveyard said. "You can't stay here. If you don't go back to your Mum and Dad, they'll take you away and put you in a home, and you wouldn't like that would you?" The boy was silent for a moment, thinking about it. "Look," Aveyard said, "if the lead pinching is bothering you, you can forget about that. It was a damn silly thing to do, but you were not responsible. You were led astray by the other lads and so far as the police are concerned, you can forget all about the lead ..."

"As long as you promise never to do anything like that again," Bruton said. Aveyard looked up at him. Good old Jim Bruton, an eye for an eye, justice must be done! He was right, of course. They couldn't just let the lad off scot free; they couldn't encourage him down the slippery path of petty crime. But first things first; get the boy home, get him back to his mother, get him out of that attic and away from Olive Abbott and the misery of a life apart from life.

"Anyway," Bert said, "he's not my Dad!"

"I know that," Bill Aveyard said.


Bruton had taken the boy home. "Care to tell me about it, Olive?" Aveyard said, sitting downstairs by the fire, gazing into the flames. On the table was the opuntia he'd brought from the attic where it had been set in a pot beside the railway lines. The opuntia was damaged down two sides. With it he'd placed a broken plant-pot which contained a withered stump of a flower and a metal label.

"You're a wise young man," she said, "not like that other.

Oh, he's all right, but it's all dust and feathers with him ...
But you, well, you look a bit beyond."

"Your son, Peter Abbott. Supposed to be killed at Dunkirk.
He wasn't killed, was he? He came home from Dunkirk, and
you hid him in the attic. Every week, you bought food for him,
and when he started to smoke, you bought him cigarettes. Fifty,
sixty, eighty a week. I saw the ash-trays upstairs; but you're too
old to go up there any more, to clean. You can get up there,
when you have to, but it takes an effort. One night your son,
whatever his reasons were we'll never know, your son Peter
went out into the village. At night. And he saw a girl, Amy
Dunkley. He hadn't seen a girl for a long long time, and I
suppose human nature got the better of him!"

"It's allus been a man's way," Olive said, "tek what he wants
when he wants it."

"Amy Dunkley had a child. Bert, they called him. Your son
told you what he'd done, but when the child was born, you
knew anyway, without being told. All Bert's life, you've treated
him like a grandmother, not like a stranger ..."

"From the first moment they let me hold him, I knew he
was my flesh and blood!"

"Well now we come to a night about two weeks ago. A man
and a cactus, an opuntia. And also a plant called an Adonis.
Like most people who keep a greenhouse of potted plants, your
son Peter had a plant on a plank. Well, he had a few on a beam
off the floor, and one of them was an Adonis. He was reaching
up to get the Adonis off the beam when he slipped, or perhaps
the plant pot broke, but anyway, I imagine he had a heart
attack, and fell down. We know he was in a bad way physically,
overweight, and with rheumatism! I imagine reaching up like
that, and the shock of that plant falling, were enough to finish
him. He died of a heart attack and fell. On his way down, his
hands rubbed the side of the opuntia ..."

"Came from Arizona, that cactus did. I bought it for him,
oh years ago now, in the flower show in Wellingborough, from
some people called Collis, years ago now. And he was proud of
it, and looked after it all through the years. 'Come on, Ma,' he
used to say to me, 'doesn't that make you think of Arizona?'
and I used to sit with him by the railway line, and we'd set

185

off for Arizona together, through the desert, through the cactusses ..."

"We're not in the desert now, Olive," Aveyard said gently, "we're in your attic, and your son's lying on the floor after his heart attack. What could you do? You couldn't take him outside and dig a grave for him ... There was no way you could dispose of your son's body, was there? But then you had a lucky inspiration, you remembered the Guy Fawkes!"

"I had to sew him inside the Guy. I hadn't any alternative ..."

"You took his legs and dragged him downstairs. That wouldn't be too difficult, drag him downstairs, sew the clothing of the Guy all round him, tight as could be, then wait for the Bragg boys to come and take him away. And for a final touch, since he was your son, and you'd loved him, and everyone else was against him, and tried to crucify him by making him a soldier, you wound the wire round his head!"

"Dust to dust, ashes to ashes. It didn't matter. He was dead. The fire could have him, the fire could save him ..."

"When we were called into the Dunkley house, suddenly you realised that though your son may be dead, your grandson was still alive and could take his place up there in the attic."

"You know what they call that Adonis plant," Olive said, suddenly cackling. "The Pheasant's Eye! My son, my boy, as they wanted to take away from me, and make him a soldier, and killing people when he didn't want to kill nobody, him and me we used to travel through the fields and the forests and the mountains and deserts, together, allus together, and he'd say, 'look, Ma, we're going through Arizona', or 'see the Pheasant's Eye, Ma, it's looking at you', and I kept him with me, right to the end, until he found death where he'd been looking all them years, death, in a pheasant's eye!"

Aveyard got up to go.

"Do you think they'll put me away?" Olive asked.

"No, I don't think they'll do that," Aveyard said.

# CHAPTER THIRTY-ONE

Superintendent Bill Aveyard and Sergeant Jim Bruton left the village school of Ulton together. Already the tea-making machine, the typewriters and the copiers were being loaded into the furniture van. The typists had gone home to a late Sunday tea, Inspector Coates to sleep at last, the Detective Chief Superintendent to finish planting his rose bushes. Blatsoe had confessed to stealing the pheasants.

"We shan't get a case," Aveyard said, "Newsome'll never prosecute."

Sunday evening in the village, and for the hundredth, or is it the thousandth time, the Reverend Francis Elk wonders if he's done right to change the inside of the Church. Jo Elks feeds him, worries for him, loves him. "God's will be done," she says and her simplicity reassures him.

Aubrey Bollard's taken a bath, sprayed himself with deodorant, borrowed one of Jimmy's ties. "Don't wait up for me, Dad," he says, "I may be late!"

"Where is it tonight, pictures in Birton?"

Jimmy punches Aubrey affectionately. "Our big brother's got a date," he says, "he's taking Iris Latham to a disco ..."

"Dens of iniquity," Tom Bollard says, but he's glad Aubrey's 'spreading his wings'.

Benny Latham was sitting in the front room of his cottage, two rooms downstairs, three bedrooms, stone built with a thatched roof. He was adding the money in his Trustees Savings Bank Book, and referring to a gardening catalogue. There was enough in the Savings Bank for a greenhouse; but if he could wait until he'd sold all the bulbs now making roots in pots in his present greenhouse, he'd have sufficient cash to buy a proper heating and ventilating system to go with it. Aye, and perhaps a mist propagator!

Stephany Latham came into the front room. "Mr Western came," she said.

"Good!" Benny Latham put down his savings book, took up the catalogue. "Look at what they're doing now!" he said. "Freezing chrysanthemums so's you can bring 'em into flower any time you want ...!"

"You and your flowers!" she said. "Sometimes I wonder if that's all you think about!"

He grabbed her to him. "You know that's not right," he said, "and you've got kids to prove it!" She hugged him close, embarrassed by his sudden show of affection. "It's nice, isn't it," she said, "our Iris being asked out by Aubrey. He's coming to fetch her, an' all. I hope you'll shave!"

"It's not me he's taking out! Anyway, what's so special about a blacksmith's lad! Next year, you mark my words, she'll be the daughter of a market gardener!"

Sunday evening; Aveyard and Bruton tell the driver to follow and walk through the village.

"Interesting case, legally," Aveyard says.

When the Chief accused Brian Sharp, after finding a jacket with crystals on the lining where the arsenic solution had evaporated, Brian Sharp confessed to the petty crime of stealing *objets d'art* from various village cottages, he confessed to wishing Stanley Robinson were dead and having done something about it. "Freely, frankly, and of sound mind," he said, "I confess I meant to have a go at *Stanley* Robinson!"

But it was Helen Robinson who had the hypo stuck in her back, by accident.

"Does that make it an accidental death?" Jim Bruton asked, musing as they walked slowly along Church Street, towards Tingdene Way.

"It'll be a marvellous case for the prosecuting office to get its teeth into ..."

"*That's* why you asked the Chief to go! I wondered why you didn't want the satisfaction of 'doing' Brian Sharp yourself."

"That prosecuting office! Too much paper work for me, and you know how I hate paper work!" Aveyard said.

Sunday evening and Stanley Robinson released from custody

returned to an empty house, cleared once again of suspicion of murder. He stood in his greenhouse, a cup of tea in his hands, looking at his plants. Automatically he reached for a piece of cane with which to stir the tea but then put down the cane, remembering.

The police told him they'd made an arrest in connection with the death of his wife; they gave him an outline of the motive and let him see the letter his wife had written, since eventually it would be read in a public court of law as evidence. This much only was important to him; for reasons of her own, and there's no accounting for a woman's tastes, his wife had preferred Brian Sharp to himself.

He seated himself on a bent-wood chair, turned an early chrysanthemum flower so he could look into its centre. "Nature's still wonderful, man's still vile!" he said out loud.

Aveyard and Bruton passed at the end of Tingdene Way; the Wolseley driving slowly behind them stopped, awaiting instructions.

"Arthur Newsome'll never agree to a prosecution!" Aveyard said.

"I don't suppose he will. He'll carry on as before, I expect, going shooting three times a week, but somehow he'll contrive never to speak to Blatsoe directly!"

"Stanley Robinson'll have arrived home. I'd like to see him before we pack up, just call in ..."

"It can't be good coming home to a house as empty as that one," Bruton said, thinking of his own fireside. He beckoned to the Wolseley driver. "That new estate, Eastfields. I'll tell you where to stop," he said, as they got in the back.

"I'd still like to know what John Western was doing at the Latham cottage," Aveyard said. "What do you think it was?"

"I haven't the faintest idea. It didn't show up in any of the statements ..."

"You and your statements ..."

The car drew up outside Robinson's gate; they walked down the path and Bruton knocked on the door. "Keeps a clean garden," he said, looking round. "Not a weed anywhere." There was no reply to his knock. "He can't be home yet," he said, as they walked back up the path to the car.

189

"I'll pop out this evening," Aveyard said. "So far as I know, dammit, I'm not doing anything else."

Stanley Robinson drank half the cup of tea, tipped a tablespoonful of what the police had called Sample 'A' into the rest of it, and drained the cup in one quick gulp.

When the arsenic took effect he jerked upright in the first spasm of pain; the chair on which he had been sitting toppled over, and his hands clutched a Chrysanthemum and the Cleistocactus Straussii as he fell across the staging of the greenhouse, then rolled to the floor.

*If you have enjoyed this book, you might
wish to join the Walker British Mystery Society.*

*For information, please send a postcard or
letter to:*

**Paperback Mystery Editor**

**Walker & Company
720 Fifth Avenue
New York, NY 10019**